THE WORLD OF
SUPERSAI

RAPTORS OF PARADISE

JAY JAY BURRIDGE

Ⓢ

First published in Great Britain in 2017 by
Supersaurs
80-81 Wimpole Street, London, W1G 9RE
www.supersaurs.com

A CIP catalogue record for this book is available from the British Library.

ISBN: 978–1–786–96801–2

Typeset in Adobe Jenson by Perfect Bound Ltd
Printed and bound by Page Bros, Norwich

Supersaurs is an imprint of Bonnier Zaffre,
a Bonnier Publishing Company
www.bonnierpublishing.co.uk

For Mouse, Bear and Fox
and all the other creatures in my life.

Rouib
inui
Muka
Beari
Banana
Pope
Htt Strait
Salwatty
Saylee
Kanary
Mysol
Bebe
Wauwu

Dorey
Raptors of Paradise
Mt. Allen

Dorey Har.
Mansinam
Sook
Biak
Mafor
Jobie
Amberpoca

Maciuer Inlet

GUINEA

Warou
Wawowerus
Kibwaru
Toho
Kessing
Certier.iam
Goram
Matabello I.
Teor
Boen
Triton

Panua Kanaii

5

Dobbo

Aru I.s

Vorka

little Key

Mose
Tenemboi
Niba
Iesat

Daai

M Plash

Timor Laut

100 fathom line

Christopher West   The Sauria Trading Company   1912 London England

Somewhere Deep
in the Rainforest

Morning was well underway when a man entered the rainforest clearing and picked up a mottled, dark grey feather. He then inspected the sight hanging limply from a rope before him. Upside down and suspended by one leg, the large feathered form spun slowly round and round, its one free leg revealing its razor-sharp foreclaw. Finally the man focused on its staring ice-blue eyes.

The man bent down and peered more closely. Without warning, the raptor lunged, snapping its strong jaws, forcing him to fall backwards and scream in shock.

'You OK back there?' came a gruff voice.

'Sorry, boss. It's still alive!' The man took out his revolver. 'Shall I kill it?'

'No. I want that one alive . . .'

I

Arrival By Boat

~ after doing a lot of nothing ~

Koto Baru, Wokan, the Islands of Aru,
Maluku province of Eastern Indonesia, 1932

Beatrice Kingsley woke with a start in a tangle of rope and old canvas. The *Orca's* engines had changed pitch, which meant the small but heavily laden steamer boat was slowing, which meant . . . land! She sat up smartly, rubbing her face and blinking sleep out of her eyes as she peered out at the moonless night. Blackness engulfed everything except the stars above and the lights onboard the *Orca*, but the unmistakable hot, wet smell of forest coming from the approaching island filled her nostrils. It was intoxicating.

'Bea, you awake?' came a rumbling call from the wheelhouse.

'Yes, Captain!' She leapt up the steps in bare feet to where Captain Woods stood illuminated by the dim light of his map table.

'Aye, thought you might be. Make yourself useful, will you?' He pointed at a long coil of heavy rope. 'I'll bring us in, but I need you to hop down to the dock – don't fall in – and make fast the other end of that line to something solid.'

The *Orca* slowly drew closer to the rickety old jetty. A lantern hung lazily off the boat's rail, but the night's blackness was gradually giving way to the grey light that washes everything down before the dawn. Bea went as far forward as she could, one foot resting on the rail, ready to take a leap.

'I can't see much from here, Bea. You guide me in.'

'Steady as she goes, Captain, we're nearly there,' Bea called back. 'I'll go in three . . . two . . .' She dropped noiselessly to the wooden planks, rope in hand, and looped it round a post, taking the strain as the boat gently came alongside. They had finally arrived.

'Great job, Bea. Make a bowline there and I'll toss down the aft line when you're ready.'

Two minutes later, the *Orca* safely docked, Bea dusted her hands off on her gingham skirt and turned to look down the jetty. It was a relief to be on dry land. Two days and nights in close quarters aboard the *Orca* from Papua had been just about bearable but now Bea was eager to explore. She wanted to make the most of her time off the boat. They were only at the halfway point of their trip: they would have to do it all over again to get home to England.

'Not bad for a landlubber. You're a damn sight better than my lazy lot.' Captain Woods held out his hand to help her back onboard.

'Shall I wake everyone and let them know we're here?' Bea asked.

'Leave 'em to their beauty sleep. Nothing's going to happen for a while. In fact, I've got some snoring to catch up on myself – I suggest you do the same.'

The captain swung himself into his hammock in one fluid movement, then tilted his hat over his face. True to his word, he was asleep in moments.

Bea was wide awake, though, and thought it best to make herself useful. Her bags, along with her grandmother's and Theodore's, had been the last to be loaded so would need to be the first off the boat, so she got to work. Her luggage was simple and lightweight: one small case for a few changes of sensible clothes, plus her riding clothes and boots in case she got the chance to do what she wanted for once and found someone with an allosaur she could ride. Bea had, with great satisfaction, conspired to lose a second large case early on in the trip, which had been stuffed with pretty frocks and formal dresses. Her grandmother, Bunty, had made her pack them, but they were far too silly to wear while running or riding.

Bea excelled at biology, science and art at school, and had been commissioned by her grandmother to be the official illustrator and recorder of facts for this trip. Bea's passions were no surprise, having been brought up looking at her father's library of books containing all sorts of information, diagrams and illustrations. Her friends often teased her for her lack of interest in fashionable novels and school gossip; Bea always opted to be the purveyor of factual information only. Her satchel contained her tools of the trade: a notebook; a larger sketchbook already filled with colourful drawings; and her well-used pencil case with its hole that badly needed sewing up. There was also a roll of string with pre-marked lines on for measurements and some glue in case anything needed sticking down. Finally there was a tin case containing brushes and watercolour paints to bring her drawings to life.

Bea's grandmother Bunty had a different approach to packing. Each of her three travel trunks was big enough to climb into and contained a bewildering array of corsets, petticoats and hats. This was apparently 'travelling light' but as Bea was often reminded 'you never know what to expect'. Judging by the sheer weight of the cases, Bunty was expecting anything up to and including the apocalypse. She'd want to have the right hat for the occasion.

Bunty Brownlee had set up a very successful saur stud farm with her husband, the late Sidney Brownlee, in America. When Sidney died Bunty had returned to England to manage his old Oxfordshire estate, then subsequently turned the farm they owned in Kenya into a safari lodge where people could observe some of the last White Titan Tyrants in the wild. She was very used to hot climates and mucking in with the men, but did not see that as an excuse to let standards slip.

Last of all there was Theodore Logan's kit: one old and battered army-issue bag that contained his entire life. If Theodore did have a change of clothes in it, the fresh outfit would be identical to what he always wore. He certainly didn't seem to have added much clothing since Bea had known him. It was possible he slept in his cowboy hat.

The most important items for Theodore were his knife, hat and gun – in that order – followed by all kinds of survival and first-aid equipment. He had fought in the First World War and had learnt some particularly tough lessons along the way, taking Bunty's saying 'you never know what to expect' to a whole new level of preparedness. Theodore had worked for Bunty and Sidney ever since they had found him as a skinny young stowaway, escaping the hard grey life of London's docks and heading for the promise of a new world – America. Now more of a cockney cowboy than an urchin, Theodore was a solid, reliable presence for the two women in his life.

Bea found a broken sack trolley on the dockside to stack their cases and perched on top, dangling her feet as she watched the dawn. At first the early light made a silhouette of the island at the other end of the jetty and then, as the sun finally popped above the low horizon, it drenched Bea and the *Orca* in a pool of molten gold, moving up the jetty one plank at a time and then on to the small town behind her.

A couple of crew emerged from below deck with a stretch and a yawn. They tiptoed past the snoring captain and poured the coffee that Bea had made, nodding their thanks for a hot cup, a quiet dock and a sleeping boss. All good things must come to an end, though, and when Captain Woods sat up so quickly he fell out of his hammock with a yell, Bea knew that Bunty was coming on deck.

'Good morning, Captain. What are you doing lying under your hammock? Ah, Beatrice, darling, there you are. Be a good girl and fetch a porter.'

'I don't think it's that sort of port, Grandma,' said Bea, gesturing at the empty dock, as the young deckhand passed Bunty a cup of coffee and ducked out of her way quickly.

'Of course it is. All ports have porters, you need only apply yourself to the problem. And would it have troubled you too much to help out?' Bunty went on. 'You could have made this coffee instead of sitting around waiting on our bags. At least the crew have been busy.'

Bea opened her mouth to say something about the injustice then shut it again. She thought it best not to rock the boat – not first thing in the morning, at least. Instead, she grumpily pulled out her note pad and wrote: '1: NEVER make everyone coffee again.'

Theodore Logan ducked cautiously through the cabin door. The *Orca* was definitely built for smaller people. He waved his hat at Bea and followed his nose to the coffee pot.

'That smells like my kind of brew. Looks like you chaps are finally getting the hang of proper coffee.' He shook the captain's hand. 'Wilbur. Thanks for the ride, mate – we'll get out of your hair now. We should be ready to leave again in a few days, as arranged.'

People instinctively liked Theodore Logan, and Captain Woods was no exception. They had shared a dram or two of Theodore's prized single malt whiskey over the last few nights, and the captain had produced a few intoxicating bottles of rum – this combination had led to a very good-natured scars-and-storytelling competition. As far as Bea was concerned, however, she and Bunty had passed the sea voyage doing a lot of nothing.

Theodore hastened over to Bunty to help her step from the boat to the jetty, waving away the slender-framed deckhand.

'I'll take over from here. You've done enough already – those bags are heavier than they look, eh? Bea, look after Bunty while I go and get us a porter, will you?' With that, Theodore strode off purposefully.

As Bea looked around the deserted port, she couldn't help thinking that their arrival at the Islands of Aru, the final destination on this epic slog of a trip, was the biggest anticlimax that she had ever encountered. Her summer holidays should have been spent having fun with her friends in the lush Oxfordshire countryside, and riding her beloved allosaur, Rusty. Not being dragged halfway around the world to the Spice Islands by way of many, many different trains, planes and automobiles and finally the *Orca*, a smelly cramped cargo boat. But here they were: Grandma, needing help off a boat, as ever; Theodore, who followed Bunty around the world making sure she stepped off boats properly; and Bea. She wrote: '2: NEVER going on a boat again,' then, a minute later, added in brackets '(unless on a boat going home).'

Bea sighed. This was turning into one of those days. Bea loved Bunty and Theodore dearly, but they could be so infuriating sometimes and they never consulted her about important decisions. The whole trip had been sprung on her only a month ago. Bunty had said it would be a good opportunity to see the many exotic creatures and locations that filled the pages of her father's books, but the extraordinary hassle in getting here had made it hard to enjoy. Bea sighed again. Sometimes she missed having real parents more than she could bear.

Bunty, sensing Bea's mood, attempted to cheer her granddaughter up. 'Remember that delightful feather

bonnet that your great-auntie Geraldine gave you? The one that was sadly lost with your other case? Well, it came from right here.'

'I thought it was from a shop in Burlington Arcade in London,' Bea said sulkily.

'Yes, well, that's where the hat came from, but those feathers came all the way from here. Quite remarkable. Perhaps if we're lucky we might see some of those Raptors of Paradise while we're here. You could collect enough feathers to make your own bonnet when we get home.'

'I can't wait,' said Bea with finality.

After a few minutes, Theodore strode back up the jetty.

'Good news, a porter of sorts is on his way. No idea when he'll get here. Rather than waiting, we should leave our cases here and look about town. I'll get the captain to keep an eye on our stuff. Also, Bunty . . . the post office is just up the road.'

'I'd rather stay here,' Bea said quickly. She just wanted some time on her own.

Theodore and Bunty looked at each other for a moment then replied in stereo: 'Great!'

'Really?' Bea was confused. They never agreed with her plans.

'Absolutely, my darling,' said Bunty. 'You stay and wait for the porter. We won't be long. I could do with stretching my legs and posting a letter before it gets too hot.' Bunty smiled at Bea a little too brightly, popped her parasol open and took Logan's proffered arm.

Bea watched them go with a slight frown. Something was definitely up.

2

Eleven Years Late

*~ the Spice Island Post always
delivers ~*

Walking briskly, Theodore and Bunty followed the sounds, smells and widening dusty road that led into town. Most of the locals momentarily stopped their daily morning tasks to take note of the island's newest arrivals. Bunty smiled at a child who was trying to help his father heap a freshly cut pile of palm leaves into a small nesting paddock housing a pair of silver shorthorn tritops. Without the boy realising, the leaves were landing on an exotic-looking oviraptor who was desperately trying to nudge her many younglings out of the way. As they continued walking a repetitive thumping sound grew louder. As they turned a corner Theodore quickly told Bunty to turn away. Too late – Bunty saw for herself the butcher hacking away at the carcass of a tritops calf, blood splattering its delicate silvery skin and spilling into a metal pan under the table.

Bunty was starting to feel the heat.

'Shall we get some water, Theodore?' she asked, indicating a hadrosaur with two large leaking barrels strapped to its sides waiting patiently alongside its owner.

Theodore muttered to Bunty under his breath, 'That water delivery service probably comes from the same spring that the hadrosaurs wallow in. There's a reason the bar serves liquor all day – less chance of serious illness,' and he tapped the water can attached to his belt as a way of saying that he already had their needs covered. Bunty accepted a drink from Theodore gratefully.

Thankfully when they reached the post office there were no signs of either slaughter or infection, but it did have a 'closed' sign hanging on the door. Theodore remained outside, but Bunty chose to ignore the sign and turned the handle.

The door creaked as she entered, accompanied by a razor-sharp slice of sunlight that scored a sudden bright line across the floor. Bunty brought with her a very faint

scent of roses, rare in the wet heat of the Islands of Aru. She stepped purposefully to the counter. Squaring her shoulders, she puffed her cheeks out, touched her necklace for luck and dinged the bell. It didn't so much 'ding' as 'dink', but the sound provoked a sudden explosion of noise from the shadows behind the counter.

'What sort of a tree-brained buffoon are you if you can't even let a poor old lady like me have my morning contemplation in peace? Touch that bell again and I'll do more than just twist your nose!'

Unable to resist the temptation, Bunty gave the bell another firm *dink* and then stepped back to see what would happen. She wasn't disappointed.

From behind the counter erupted a mass of bright feathers stuck into jet black, tightly curled hair, accompanied by a torrent of swear words and insults in at least five different languages.

Instead of a tree-faced buffoon on the other side of her counter, the postmistress (for that was who it was) found a sturdy English lady dressed head to toe in sensible travelling clothes, with an umbrella hanging on one folded arm and giving her an amused gaze from below her sun hat. The postmistress squawked, disappeared once more from view behind the counter and, after a few seconds rustling and a few muffled curses, re-emerged with a blue smock, a badge that said 'International Spice Island Postal Service' and an official-looking hat that set off the feathers in her hair rather well.

'Ahem. H'apologies for the temporary disruption to our service, madam. How may I be of assistance?'

'Good morning,' said Bunty. 'I am sorry to have woken you, I just couldn't resist ringing the bell again.'

'Not at all, not at all. I'm just glad you aren't that miserable excuse for a son, Shuggy. He's always eating candied ginger and ringing bells when he should be helping his poor mother with the chores. Are you new to the island? I have some rooms for rent if you like?'

Bunty had seen the 'Rooms For Rent' sign outside but had already decided that this was not a suitable option.

'Thank you, but that won't be necessary. I'm rather hoping you might be able to help me. You see, I received a letter.'

'Well, you came to the right place, my lovely. Post Office and General Store is the best place to come when you got a letter.'

'Yes, well, you see, it's not just any letter. And I have already received it – I mean, it was posted to me – at home, in England.'

'England, you say? My, my, how is that handsome king? Got a couple of his stamps right here, I have.'

Bunty shook her head 'Oh, he's very well, thank you, I'm sure, but . . . oh, I'm not really making myself clear. You see, the letter was from my daughter, Grace. And I'm trying to find her. And the postmark – I mean, it only arrived a month ago and I came straight away, but she sent it eleven years ago. Please look,' said Bunty, reaching into her pocket and pulling out a much-handled, worn old envelope, covered in scuffs and stamps. 'The letter says February 1921.'

A big smile took over the postmistress's face. 'Madam, this is an honour! I send many letters to your country but I never seen one come back with a person attached. Where are my manners? Come, sit here on my office chair so we can have a proper look at this.'

All good post offices have a magnifying glass, and the Spice Island Head Office was no exception. The postmistress kept hers – a beautiful ebony-handled one that looked at least as old as she was – on a heavy cord around her neck. Once installed next to Bunty at the desk, she put the glass over her eye and bent over the envelope, muttering as she scrutinised it.

Eventually she sat up, straightened her hat and said, 'Yes, Lady Brownlee, this letter did indeed originate from here. It must have been left here many years ago, but only reached me by accident in my official capacity as post-handler about four or five months ago.'

'Oh, my. You see,' said Bunty impatiently, her voice giving an uncharacteristic wobble, 'I'm trying to find out what happened to it.'

'What happened? My dear, it got sent to you, and then you brought it here. It's right here on my counter. Oh, don't look so upset.' She patted Bunty on the hand. 'Look, you've come a long way, it's hot and you're vexed. Why don't you tell me again from the beginning and we'll fix it together.'

The postmistress realised that something important might be afoot. So she removed her official hat, replaced a few feathers in her hair and the two of them got down to business.

'Now, this letter. This is why you're here?'

'Yes.'

'And it's late?'

'Indeed. By eleven years.'

'And you come here to register a complaint or something?'

'No, no. Well, not to you specifically. You see, I want to know *why* it was delayed. My daughter sent it to me – it's dated shortly after she and her husband disappeared. And until I got this, I thought I'd never hear from her again. It gave us hope. I daren't tell my granddaughter – she just thinks we are here to see the wildlife. My husband's friend Theodore and I – he's outside – we've been all over the world for the past eleven years trying to find out what happened to them.'

'And now you're here.'

'Indeed. And now we're here.'

'Oh, my poor, poor dear. No wonder you were all in a worry. Well, look, I'm afraid there's not a lot I can help you with. You see, we'd never have found it in the first place if Shuggy hadn't fallen off the ladder.'

'I beg your pardon?'

'The ladder, the one in the back. You see, the old postmaster was . . . eaten and I took over 'bout five years ago. And it was found in an old tin next to where I'd hidden Shuggy's candied ginger. The little rapscallion snuck down in the night to steal a little snack, only he knocked that tin over, fell off the ladder and near broke his arm. I come downstairs with my old machete thinking him a burglar and fixing to chop him up into little pieces – LITTLE PIECES, SHUGGY!' she suddenly yelled into the back of the office.

'Right. And the tin was . . .?'

'Next to the ginger on the floor. It opened when it fell and the ginger jar broke – and out came this old unsent letter. So I sent it to you with extra stamps out of my own pocket to make it arrive double-quick.' She paused and nodded once before concluding, 'I'm the postmistress.'

Bunty dug around for the appropriate response, before settling on, 'Gosh, well, do I owe you anything for the extra stamps? They are rather fine.'

'No, no! It might be late, but the Spice Island Post always delivers.'

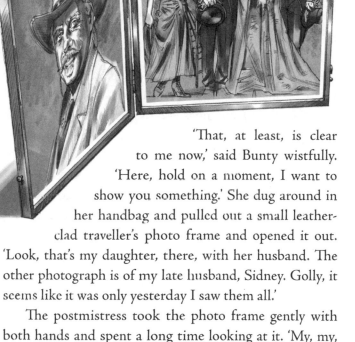

'That, at least, is clear to me now,' said Bunty wistfully. 'Here, hold on a moment, I want to show you something.' She dug around in her handbag and pulled out a small leather-clad traveller's photo frame and opened it out. 'Look, that's my daughter, there, with her husband. The other photograph is of my late husband, Sidney. Golly, it seems like it was only yesterday I saw them all.'

The postmistress took the photo frame gently with both hands and spent a long time looking at it. 'My, my, she look pretty. She look like you. What a beautiful wedding dress. Like something from a dream. Crazy for a place like this, but beautiful. I'm so sorry I can't help you. What will you do now?'

Bunty put the photo frame back in her bag, allowing herself to stroke it once. She smiled bravely. 'Well, it seems mad to come all this way and not experience the jungle. Theodore is looking for a guide and we'll see if we can't spot a few of your famous Raptors of Paradise. We'll do that and then head for home. This was our last hope. Thank you so much for listening – and sorry to have disturbed you.'

She turned and was almost at the door when the postmistress called her back. 'Hold on, madam. Maybe you're asking the wrong person. Look – turn right out of here and go a few buildings over by the depot.' She pointed through the window. 'Ask for Hayter. He's probably sulking up in his office.'

'Really? Who's Hayter?'

'Hayter likes to think he's in charge around here, lets people know it too. He like a leech sucking the life out of everyone around here.' She growled under her breath. 'Right piece of work, he is – nothing gets on or off this island that he don't know about. Probably already know you're here too. Probably already upset you ain't seen him first.'

Bunty shielded her eyes from the sun and looked at the depot for a moment. 'What do they do there?' Bunty asked.

'You'll find out as soon as you enter. Him been taking from this island for years and years now, god knows what he does with it all. Anyhow, me must get back to Shuggy and the letters. They won't send themselves!' She winked.

'Thank you so much again. I'll go and see if this Mr Hayter can help. Goodbye.'

Bunty went to find Theodore where he waited in the shade, squatting next to a couple of cages with a canteen of water in his hand.

'Hello,' he said. 'Any luck?'

'Not really.' Bunty sighed. 'Lovely lady and desperate to help, but it was all before her time as postmistress. She only found the letter by accident. I have been staring at the post box every day for eleven years wondering why the letters stopped. I haven't stopped thinking about it.' Bunty sighed again, then said, 'What on earth is that strange-looking saur?'

Theodore bent down and faced the creature inside the cage. 'Saw one of these in Australia. It's a cassowary. Looks harmless but had quite a temper, and very sharp claws.'

'Are you sure it's not one of those odd short-tailed oviraptors we saw this morning?' Bunty asked.

Theodore filled one hand with a splash of water and offered it through the bars to the hot-looking beast. 'Quite sure. That was a cassabanji. They mimic these indigenous vicious birds so that bigger creatures think twice to attack them.' Theodore had kept talking as he could sense the forthcoming news was a disappointment, but now he had to ask. 'Did the postmistress explain why the letter took so long to arrive? If it had arrived earlier it might have saved me looking for them all over Australia for a year.'

Bunty eyed up the corrugated tin roof of the dilapidated old post office and then turned towards the depot up the road. 'Shuggy stole some ginger and fell off a ladder. Look, this is probably the last place on the trail – but we don't even know for sure if it was Gracie who posted the letter here. It could have been someone else.'

'And may I ask who Shuggy is?' Theodore said, puzzled, as the cassowary drank from his hand.

'Forget Shuggy,' Bunty replied. 'The real question is: who's Hayter? And what's in his depot? The postmistress says he's not a nice man, but he might be able to help. We can pop in to see him and then go and find Beatrice. Care to join me, good sir?'

'Delighted,' murmured Theodore with a smile and, holding out an arm for Bunty, the two of them strolled up the dusty road as if promenading round Hyde Park on a Sunday morning.

3

Christian Hayter

~ that dreadful little man ~

Amongst the shacks and huts that lined the muddy red dirt track that was the town's main road, the depot loomed large, its tall wooden walls burned black by the sun. The main building had a couple of small, filthy windows right up under the eaves of the tin roof, amongst its many missing sections, but no other distinguishing features except for a peeling sign above the doors that read:

Trading Depot. Est. 1922.
Christian Hayter – Serving The Community.

Underneath, some joker had added the words: 'on a plate'. Outside, near a pile of empty cages and a mound of soiled sawdust, two hot-looking mimusaurs, saddled and ready to go, were tethered to the sturdy fence posts that ran around most of the building.

From inside they could hear the chatter and squawk of innumerable animals – and the closer they got, the stronger the smell of the place grew. Bunty balled her

linen handkerchief in front of her nose but pressed on. For Theodore, who had grown up in a butcher's yard, it was nothing new. He stepped ahead and was just about to knock when they heard a sudden scream from inside. A human scream.

This was immediately followed by another at a higher pitch and then someone shouted 'GET IT!' A clattering and stamping of feet from one side of the depot to the other sent puffs of dust out through the boards. Something big thumped the other side of the thin wooden wall, shaking the sign on the front of the rickety building. The tethered mimus tried to back away but were held by their reins.

'Sit on it! Pin it down, you fools!' The air was suddenly filled with the high shriek of an animal in distress. Then came a tearing noise – splintering wood – that made the mimus, Theodore and Bunty all wince. Whatever the struggle was, it was clearly not over yet.

From within came another cry – 'Ah! It got me!' – followed by a stream of curses that made Bunty raise an eyebrow. Suddenly the doors slammed open, sending the skittish mimus into a panic. Two men flew out, rolling over and over in the dust, bringing a heavy stench of meat with them. One was clearly in a bad way, bleeding heavily from a gash across his forehead.

His red-haired companion bent over him and clasped his head roughly in his hands before pronouncing: 'Just a couple of stitches, that's all. You'll be fine.'

Bunty tapped him on the shoulder. 'Excuse me. Mr Hayter?'

'Not me, love, no. The gaffer's inside. He'll be the one who's still standing. Come on, Bishop, let's get you fixed up.'

As the two men dusted themselves down and hobbled off, Logan took Bunty by the elbow and said, 'You know, I think it might be best if just this once you let me take the lead when we get inside.'

'Of course, Theodore. I'm finding it hard enough to breathe, let alone talk.' The stink of damp fur and feathers had become stronger and was now mixed with the eye-watering ammonia bite of animal dung.

The squawking and hissing suddenly stopped and became muffled, then a voice shouted urgently from within: 'Rope! Pass me the rope! Bishop, Ash, you clowns – where are you?'

Never one to leave a person in need, Theodore shoved the doors open. The room was huge. Stacked wooden crates and metal cages of all sizes lined the walls, each of which contained something that was trying to get out. In the middle, kneeling in a single shaft of bright light from the small windows, was a short, stocky man holding under one arm a large, greyish raptor in a painful-looking headlock. The saur had a leg free and was thrashing about, gouging deep scratch marks into the pitted wooden floor with its fore claw, desperate for enough purchase to lift itself up. Both saur and human were quivering with exhaustion and in need of help.

'Whoever you are you'll do! Rope – get some rope!'

Theodore followed the man's eyes and saw a coil of rope next to an upturned desk. He quickly measured out a couple of yards, unsheathed his Bowie knife and cut a length.

'Done. Ready.'

'Now lash its mouth shut. Quick.'

The raptor had loosened one of its feathered forearms from under the man's knee and started to flap as best it could to free itself, sending plumes of dust and fine feathers up into the room. The man dug his knee deep into the saur's back with enough force to hold it still. Theodore made a slipknot, dropped it over the saur's muzzle and wound it round five times.

'Now loop the tail to its snout.'

'What?' Theodore asked.

'Grab its tail and tie the end to its face,' said the man with exaggerated patience. 'It can't run away, only in circles.'

'Won't that hurt it?' Bunty asked from the safety of the doorway.

The man simply stared at her. Theodore kept quiet and made the tie, but left a few fingers' worth of slack. He didn't like this one bit, but now wasn't the right time to argue.

'Now stand well back, and hold onto the other end of the rope. You ready?'

Theodore placed himself in front of Bunty and wound the end of the rope around his forearm. Seeing this, the man stood up quickly, taking a pace backwards. The raptor, after an instant's surprise at being allowed to stand, leapt to its feet like a coiled spring, knocking the man slightly off balance. With its head tied to its ragged tail, the raptor was too confused to do much more. It would have looked funny if it didn't look so sad.

Theodore held the rope as the man stood and slowly pulled a vicious-looking weapon from his belt. It was a club about two and a half feet long, with a steel head and cruel downward-curved hook protruding from the end. With one precise, neat swing he caught one of the raptor's legs and swept its feet from under it. Then, without a moment's consideration for its razor-sharp talons, he leapt on top of it again and wrapped its legs in his strong arms.

'That's right, you just lie there,' he crooned as he dug an elbow into its thigh. 'Our new friend is going to tie your shoelaces for you.'

The man looked up at Theodore who, while he didn't agree with the methods, couldn't argue with their results, and had another loop of rope ready. It took a person of great strength, courage or complete stupidity to tackle a wild saur, and Theodore was wondering if perhaps this character might tick all three boxes.

When the task was done, Theodore offered a hand to help

the man up off the neatly trussed and incapacitated raptor.

'Well, that's quite a start to the morning.'

'Nice to meet you, mate. You saved my bacon. What do I call you?'

'Theodore Logan.'

'Christian Hayter.'

They shook once, firmly. Neither man smiled as they gauged each other. 'And this is my friend Barbara Brownlee,' offered Theodore.

'Pleased to meet you, Mr Hayter.'

'Likewise, I'm sure.' Hayter dug in his pockets for a grubby handkerchief and mopped some of the sweat and grime from his face. 'So, what brings you to my part of the world? I hope it's work you're looking for, Logan. You know your way around a saur and –' he looked around the room, 'well, I'm not sure if Ash or Bishop are sticking around for their bonus.'

Bunty started to say something, but Theodore cut in quickly. 'I know that accent. How long have you been away from London?'

'About as long as you have my friend, by the sound of it, and I don't miss the place one bit,' Hayter replied. He picked up a chair and patted the seat with his hanky, sending another cloud of dust into the air and spreading the dirt around rather than cleaning anything. 'Please sit down.' He grinned at Bunty.

'I'm fine standing, thank you,' Bunty replied, holding

her handkerchief a little closer to her nose and breathing deeply. 'Apologies if we caught you at a bad time.'

'No problem at all – I've always got time for business,' said Hayter, hauling his desk upright and wedging the door open to let in a little breeze. 'We usually only do wholesale for international markets, but you two look like collectors, and we're not above dealing direct. Cuts out the middleman – better for everyone. What was it you were after?'

'What's that?' Bunty asked, pointing to the bound heap on the floor.

'You won't want one of those. That's a shadow raptor. We usually shoot them on sight. If we see them, that is. Very good at blending in, they are. Vicious and ugly, not worth a penny. Their plumage is not a fashionable colour.'

'If it's a pest, why have you got it, then?' Bunty questioned him, as the saur looked up at her with sorry eyes.

'My pet Dwarf Black Tyrant gets hungry, and I like to treat him once a week with a kill. Best if it's fresh, don't you think? Makes a change from stinking fish and it's more fun.'

Bunty grimaced and said nothing.

Trying to edge his visitors towards a cash sale, Hayter moved over to Theodore, who was looking into one of the many cages.

'What do you reckon, Logan?'

'Well, this one certainly looks more manageable.'

'Lovely choice, my friend. Very popular this one: the Golden Fantail. Great plumage. One of the many different Raptors of Paradise from around here. The islands are full of them. We're selling more and more; they last the long journey better than the bigger ones like this one over here . . .' Hayter moved over to some larger cages. 'The Greater Raptor of Paradise, the name says it all. Normally we just pluck its two long tail feathers and chuck the rest but I have a client in Hong Kong that has a use for its green head feathers so we're picking a few up for him.'

Theodore followed him and peered into the dim cage to see a sorry-looking saur curled up in the corner, long feathers dim and matted.

'Now, I know what you're thinking, Logan,' Hayter went on. 'You're thinking "Is it worth the trip to bag a live one of these for your collection?" Well, to be honest, it's up to you. We normally slaughter them here and freeze them. They'll be stuffed back in Europe, only the generator's broken at the moment so we need to keep them alive till the parts come in.' Hayter kicked the cage and the frightened saur retreated even deeper into the corner.

'How long have you been in this trade?' asked Theodore.

'Ha! I've been fighting them all my life, earned my stripes in the Plaistow raptor pits.' Hayter grinned and looked up from under his hat brim. 'Don't look so shocked, mate. Not many people survive to say that, I can tell you –

least not with all their fingers and thumbs!'

Theodore nodded a small amount of appreciation, and corrected his earlier assumption of the man. He *definitely* ticked all three boxes.

'And how long have you been on this island?'

'Mmm, ten or so years. A Dutch man ran the trade for a long time but he lost his licence, so I stepped in.'

Theodore glanced over to Bunty. 'Then you may remember a very good friend of ours who passed by here some time back – Franklin Kingsley, an American.'

It was as if someone had shut a door in Hayter's head. Instead of having a ready reply, as he had for everything so far, his shoulders seemed to freeze. He turned away, inspecting some invisible damage on a cage.

'Sorry, mate, can't say that I do. Name don't ring any bells.' He turned back to face them, a hard look in his eyes. 'Now are you looking or buying? Only I've got work to do and this beast has already wasted a lot of my morning. Time is money, as the saying goes. Pleasure to make your acquaintance, of course.' He stood by the open door expectantly. The interview was clearly over.

Bunty took the hint, nodding politely as she brushed past him to get out. 'Thank you for your time, Mr Hayter.'

Theodore had one further question. 'Remember Logan's Saurmonger on the high street in Plaistow?'

'Ah, so you're Cockney born and bred? Logan's – how could I forget? That saurmongers had two ugly phalox

that butted me more than a few times. I thought there was
something familiar about you.'

'Those two phalox were the best thing about that place.'
Theodore's eyes flashed briefly. 'Lady and Champion are
the only things I miss from the old days. See you around,
Mr Hayter.'

'Not if I see you first, Mr Logan. And if I were you I'd
clear out sooner rather than later. There's nothing for you
here.'

Bunty and Theodore left the depot and its stench
of rotting animal behind them and headed back to the
docks. Bunty clung tighter to Theodore's arm than she
usually did.

'Well, you did that wrong, Theo.'

'What do you mean?'

'You should have helped the poor raptor and tied up
that dreadful little man instead.'

'If only, Bunty, if only. Come on, let's get back and find
Bea. We've got some planning to do.'

4

Sammy the Porter

~ nine years old, not nine years young ~

Once Bunty and Theodore had left on their errand, it hadn't taken long for the *Orca*'s crew to unload her cargo. Now the captain was installed once more in his saggy old hammock by the wheelhouse, the rest of the crew lounging in the shade on coils of rope and netting, playing card games or dozing. Crates and containers awaiting collection were stacked on the scruffy dock for the next stage of their journey.

A good deal lighter in the water than she had been when she arrived, the steamer rested well above the dockside. Someone had started to attack the streaks of dirt and grime down her sides with a scrubbing brush on a stick, but had clearly given up until the captain's snooze was nearly done. A few seagulls waddled around self-importantly, hoping to pick up some scraps of food. Perched on the *Orca*, watching from above, were some stubby-nosed pterosaurs, looking to pick up any careless seagulls that wandered too close.

Bea, sketching the scene in her sketchbook from her throne of cases, felt the coolness of someone's shadow over her shoulder and turned around. A skinny little boy dressed in an Oriental-style shirt, tatty old cut-off shorts, grubby sandals and a very worn out New York Yankees cap was grinning at her.

'Hello, I'm Sammy,' he chirped. 'Welcome to the Islands of Aru.'

Bea smiled back but didn't quite feel ready to start making friends.

'My, my, my,' the boy continued, 'you have a lot of cases for such a small person.'

'I'm not small, thank you very much. You're far smaller than me,' she replied.

'My mother has a silly trunk just like this one at home. Why you have so many? You staying for a long time?'

There were obviously going to be a lot of questions so Bea addressed the boy properly.

'I'm Bea, I'm hopefully not staying for long, and no, these are not all mine.'

'You need a porter for sure.'

'Yes, I've been told one will be here soon.'

'Yes! He is!' Sammy grabbed at the largest trunk at the bottom of the stack, yanked at it and sent the others toppling to the deck.

'Hang on! Where are you taking that? Stop this instant!' Bea was surprised to find herself stamping her foot just like her grandmother did. 'Leave it right there for the porter. Besides, it's twice your size.'

'No worries!' He kept dragging it. 'It may take me longer but I will get the job done. Plus I've got Junior for extra muscle.'

'No. You'll wait for the porter. He will be along soon, you silly child.'

Sammy stopped in his tracks and his friendly smile took on a more serious slant. 'Lady, call me silly if you want, but I am the porter. I'm nine years old, not nine years young. I've been a porter since I was six and I earn as much as my father. I own my own business and do very well at it, thank you very much. Junior, my Maximus Kylosaur, is the strongest and most handsome saur in town and he never drops his load, ever.'

Bea suddenly realised her mistake and how much she had underestimated the boy. 'I'm so sorry, Sammy, pardon me . . . you see where I come from, nine-year-old boys are all at school.'

'School? Don't worry, I already done that. How you think I know how to speak English, Dutch, Spanish and French? *Tot ziens berdank! Como estas bienvenido! Si inpossibler come on ouis seas san sellibonnier! Mondu!*'

Bea had no idea what the last bit meant but she understood that her ignorance had been made fun of in another language she did not speak. She walked over to Sammy and the case and lifted one side of it by its leather strap. He uncrossed his arms and took the other side.

'Okay, you busy bee, I will let you help me, but don't

think I'm going to tip you.' The smile came back to his face and together they began walking the trunks up the jetty.

'I'm sorry for being rude,' Bea said. 'I've had a rough few weeks getting here and, to be quite honest, I'm not sure exactly where this is or why we're here. Theodore and my grandmother never tell me anything.'

'Well, you have asked the right person, let me tell you.' Sammy paused and breathed in deeply. 'The Islands of Aru are a group of ninety-five islands. To be precise, you're now standing on Wokan. The biggest port is in Dobbo, over the waters that way. We're a bit more out of the way here in Koto Baru – the New Town. I'm told it used to be a nice place, but it's got a bit rough now. You here for some spice?' Sammy tried to look shifty and winked clumsily. 'I can get you better prices than in town.'

'No,' said Bea. 'We're here to see the Raptors of Paradise.'

'Ahh, they are very beautiful creatures.'

'That's what my grandmother keeps telling me. But the world is full of beautiful creatures – I don't understand what's so special about these?'

Sammy looked at her as he put the case down. 'Once the Islands of Aru were joined to Papua, long time ago, so we inherited some of their strange birds, saurs and other creatures that are unique to this small part of the world.'

'Yes, I read that in a book by a man called Wallace,' Bea said impatiently.

'But what the books can't show you is how they dance!' Sammy continued.

'The raptors dance?' Bea was intrigued.

'Yes, like this!' said Sammy, who then jiggled his head from left to right and held out his elbows. Bea burst out laughing, he looked so ridiculous.

Soon Bea and Sammy had re-stacked all the cases and trunks at the other end of the jetty. Sammy put a finger in each corner of his mouth and let out a shrill whistle that startled some chattering birds from the nearest tree.

'Junior!' he called into the treeline, then whistled again, emptying the rest of the neighbouring trees of wildlife. 'Junior?'

Bea was squinting at something strange half submerged in the shallows to the side of the jetty. An enormous kylosaur, easily twenty-five feet from head to tail, was enjoying the cool shaded water.

'Is this who you're looking for?' she asked.

'Junior! What you doing, it's not bath day! We've got a customer. Get out this instant.' Sammy waded into the water and climbed up the kylosaur's heavily plated back. 'Please excuse this moment, Bea. It's very embarrassing. Junior! Get out now.'

Sammy heaved on the thin harness with all his might. Eventually, and with great, almost elaborate slowness, the kylos swung its head and emerged from the shallows, water streaming off its back. Junior's true bulk was staggering:

his back was as wide as any cart and covered in rows of beautiful bony plates and spurs painted an assortment of curious colours and patterns. Along the edge the huge bony spurs made perfect handles for ropes and bags to fasten onto. He'd be a perfect carrier for heavy loads – once you pointed him in the right direction.

'I see it's not only the raptors and birds of paradise that are colourful! What lovely decoration, did you paint them yourself?' Bea asked, much to Sammy's pleasure.

Slowly Junior lumbered up the sand and finally, like an enormous playful Labrador retreiver, thumped his great tail into the water, sending up a torrent of spray that soaked Bea from head to toe.

'Junior! Stop playing with the customers, we've got bags to carry.' Sammy said. 'Let's go and do it in the shade – far too hot on the dock.'

◆ ◆ ◆

A little while later, Bea's two travelling companions walked back onto the dock. 'Well, that's definitely the good ship *Orca*,' said Bunty, looking up the jetty from underneath her parasol. 'But where on earth is Beatrice with our bags?'

Theodore uncorked his canteen and took a big glug, swilling the liquid back and forth noisily around his

mouth. He was about to spit but after a disapproving look from Bunty, swallowed it rather grudgingly. Just then a long, piercing wolf-whistle broke the dock's sleepy silence.

'Mister! Come, come! Mister! Lady! I'm Sammy the porter. Bags all loaded and ready to go, come, come! Let's talk in the shade, it's too hot for my best customers out there! Come have some coconut water – fresh and clean.'

Sammy stood on top of Junior, coconut in hand and waving so energetically he looked like he might fall off. 'Looks like we've found our bags,' said Theodore. 'Shall we get over there before he does himself an injury?'

'Excuse me, the girl who was with the cases, where is she?' Bunty enquired as she strolled over.

'Over there.' Sammy pointed out towards the water's edge where Bea was shin-deep, washing her hands in the tranquil blue.

'Is this your kylos, lad?' asked Theodore, running his hand over Junior's back and admiring his plates. 'She's a beauty. Nice paint job too.'

'Thank you, mister. Don't let him hear you say that though, he's a male. I call him Junior but his real name is Junti. My real name is Shamila but you can call me Sammy.'

'A pleasure to meet you, Sammy. I'm Bunty Brownlee, and this is my associate, Mr Theodore Logan.'

'Nice to meet you too, Lady Brownlee, Mr Wogan.'

'Logan,' corrected Theodore. 'And it's Mrs Brownlee.'

'Yes, that's what I said. Bogan.'

'I'm sure we'll work it out on the way,' said Bunty with a grin. 'Don't scowl so, Theodore, it does make you look rather silly. Sammy, I see you have met Beatrice.'

'Busy Bee, yes. Strong girl, she is. Might have a job for her, expand the business, get a mate for Junior – she could share it. She knows how to tie the right knots as well.'

Bunty looked at Sammy with a puzzled expression. 'Are you sure we're talking about the same person?'

'Her French is a bit rusty, she will have to improve – we get a lot of French here.'

Bea came over with her shoes in one hand and a pile of bleached-out shells in the other. 'Pocket, Theodore, please,' she called out in advance of her arrival. Theodore unflapped his left jacket pocket and held it open as he had done numerous times before. Theodore always had a good supply of extra pockets to hold all manner of things. In went the shells on top of a month's worth of other knick-knacks and oddments that had caught Bea's eye on the trip. At some point, probably on the long and tedious journey home, all these items would be logged and carefully drawn into her sketchbook, but for now the pocket was the best place for them.

'Beatrice, my child, Sammy here has a job offer for you – what's this all about?'

'I've said no, but it's just a tactic to get a better offer . . . and I'm not a child. I'm thirteen. Thirteen years old, not young.' Bea winked at Sammy who gave her a thumbs up.

The boy pulled himself up tall and took charge. 'Well, Mrs Lady Brownlee,' he said gravely, 'I see you already been for a walk in New Town, but you got a place to stay yet?'

'We've not made a reservation anywhere, no. What are our options?'

'Here in New Town you have only two. Number One Guesthouse, over by the bar on the main road. Not that friendly, but close enough to fall into after the bar – but you don't look like the brawling

type. Or over there, General Store and Post Office, friendly place but Shuggy lives there.'

'Ah yes. Shuggy. Say no more. Well, is there anywhere else, perhaps away from town?'

'Sure, there's the Old Town, but that's where all us old locals live. It's not fancy.' Sammy shrugged. 'Most visitors don't get that far. There's some spare huts you can use for as long as you want while you make a plan, but at least stick around for my mum's fish stew.'

'It sounds perfect,' said Bunty, using Theodore's hands and then his shoulder to climb up onto the single rope saddle on Junior's back. 'Shall we?'

5

Biggie

~ *the spice must flow* ~

The main road – the only road – was a rutted, dusty, coconut-lined avenue that meandered out of town and along the bay for about a mile. The buildings and warehouses got gradually smaller and further apart until eventually they gave way to a cluster of tin-roofed shacks around a small, natural lagoon, each raised on rickety old stilts about three feet off the ground. As they drew close a bossy rooster alerted the scattered hens that they had visitors and they darted into the shade under a hut. A young lazy hadrosaur slowly chewed the cud, trying its best to ignore the still screeching rooster next to it.

Sammy, walking ahead with Bea, turned to announce their arrival to Theodore and Bunty. 'Welcome to Koto Lama, the Old Town. The water's not as deep here and it floods sometimes, but it's got a nicer breeze here at night so we don't get mosquitoes – and the fishing is the best for miles.'

'The jungle looks closer here too,' observed Theodore.

'Yes, all the old trails go in from here. The new trade paths are wider and they go straight to port, but we keep the old ones working. Here, you two rest for a minute – looks like everyone's at work, so I've got to do some jobs quickly before they get back.'

'Can I come with you?' asked Bea.

'It would be my pleasure, come, come.'

Theodore watched the two of them scamper off together, absent-mindedly scratching Junior under his chin. Bunty, in turn, left Theodore for a moment's thought before saying: 'Come on, I've known you long enough to be able to tell something's up. Is it that Hayter character?'

Theodore paused before replying. 'Afraid so, Bunty. I thought I'd left all that a long, long way behind me, and then here of all places I don't just meet someone who's fought in the raptor pits, I help him out. It's not right.'

'I have to say, I'm a little in the dark – I don't know much about the raptor pits. Isn't it a sport or something?'

'Sport is debatable, but dark is definitely right. Humans choosing to fight each other, that's just about okay. At least they usually know what they're getting into.' Theodore adjusted his hat as he thought for a moment. 'And animals fighting each other, well, that's just an unfortunate part of nature as it happens in the wild. But humans fighting animals? It's barbaric. And that's what the raptor pits are all about. They breed raptors on so-called "farms", raising them to fight and hate humans. Then one day the raptor's cage opens and it finds itself going toe-to-toe with a human while other people stand round having a party and betting on the outcome. The people breeding them to fight aren't any better than animals themselves. I'm amazed anything gets out alive after one fight – let alone years in the ring.'

'It sounds like bear-baiting,' Bunty said sadly.

'It's worse than that,' he replied. 'Much, much worse. The raptors' claws are sharp, but their jaws are muzzled, apparently because otherwise they'd have an unfair advantage over humans. They're chained to a post in the centre of the pit so they can't leap too far, and if need be the human can retreat to the safety of the edges. The humans make up for the lack of claws with a few nasty weapons, like that bull-hook Hayter had. You can tame any large tyrants with one of those.'

Bunty shuddered. 'Who benefits from something like that?'

'Look at who profits from it. People bet big, whether they're local gangsters, bent coppers or toffs coming in to slum it. It's a massive deal in the underworld. The raptor breeders make something out of it and the villains amongst them like to play dirty to get the upper hand. Either way, the losers will always be the two in the ring – look at Hayter. He's someone with a screw loose.'

'Why haven't you mentioned anything about this before?' Bunty asked gently.

'It's not the sort of thing you can un-hear,' Theodore told her. 'I turned my back on that life and ran away from home shortly after Lady died and Champion was beaten to death by a gang of mindless thugs, which was when I met you and Sidney. Meeting Hayter has stirred some dark memories of sad times. And now I think about it, it could have been someone like Hayter who killed Champion.' Theodore's fists clenched at the thought.

'Well, I for one am very glad we did find you. Sidney, bless his soul – he and I knew you were a diamond in the rough from the start.' She lightly elbowed Theodore to get a smile out of him.

'Thank you, Bunty.' Theodore smiled back. 'I just – it was odd meeting Hayter. It would've been so easy for me to be someone like him if you hadn't saved me. I had enough run-ins with his sort back home.'

'Now don't get all sentimental, Theodore,' Bunty cut in. 'We needed a stable boy for our allosaur and it's hardly as if we paid you more than the going rate.'

'Some things haven't changed much since then.' Theodore grinned.

'Well, as far as I'm concerned you can biff Hayter on the nose as many times as you like next time you see him. Just make sure I'm there too.'

'Hayter got your back up as well, Lady B?' asked Sammy cheekily as he came out from behind one of the houses with Bea. 'He does that to most people. Mr Rogan might have to wait in line if he's got a grudge.'

'Very funny, you little squirt,' joked Theodore, aiming a half-hearted swat at Sammy's ear as the boy laughed and danced out of range. 'And it's Logan.'

Ignoring Theodore, Sammy addressed Bunty. 'How long you want to stay, Lady B? My parents will be back soon and I can clean you a room each.'

'That's kind of you to offer, Sammy, but I'm afraid Theodore and I have other plans. We want to head into the island and see your amazing Raptors of Paradise.'

Bea looked over to her grandmother. 'Already? But we've just arrived.'

'There is no time like the present, Beatrice.'

But Sammy was shaking his head. 'You sure? It takes days of trekking and even that's no guarantee.'

'We understand. We were hoping to find a guide.'

'Today? You need to get permission from Hayter first and he won't give it. No visitors, no way.' Sammy's voice became suddenly serious. 'Listen to me, people go in but don't come out.'

'Don't worry, lad,' grunted Theodore, unlashing billy cans from his pack. 'I've dealt with much worse sorts than Christian Hayter. Now, where's the closest fresh water? Need to top up for the trip.'

'You sure?' Sammy questioned again. His eyes were lit up with excitement despite the danger. No one in his life had ever shrugged away Hayter's authority with such ease. 'My father knows the paths, he can show you . . . but Hayter will be very upset. It's dangerous, lots of traps, lots of nasty surprises and spirits.'

'No one has to know we were ever in there. You leave the worrying to us. We'll speak to your old man when he gets here,' said Theodore over his shoulder as he walked to the water butt behind the houses.

✦ ✦ ✦

As the afternoon deepened, Theodore busied himself unloading the kit in Bunty's trunks that was not needed in the jungle, and then reloading it back onto Junior once he had been told that she couldn't possibly do without any of it. Grumbling, he hid one case in Sammy's house that contained only hats to prove a point upon their return. Bea kept to herself at the shoreline, painting the view and gathering more shells. Sammy ran around getting everything Bunty requested, and came up with an innovation he was particularly proud of. A woven wicker high-backed ornate chair, one of the only nice possessions in Sammy's house, was hoisted onto Junior's back and tied to a set of the saur's spikes. It looked like royalty had commanded it to be so. Bunty was impressed and pleased. She knew the trek ahead was going to be tough and she valued comfort as well as practicality.

A man was walking towards them from a gap in the treeline and when Sammy spotted this he hared off to greet him with a cheerful yell and a stream of local dialect interspersed with English. 'Biggie! Biggie! Guests!'

As the pair got closer, Bunty could see this must be Sammy's father – they had the same stride and broad grin. Sammy took care of the introductions.

'Biggie, this is Lady Bunty and Mr Logging.'

'It's Logan. Pleased to meet you, Biggie.'

'Thank you, Mr Logan. Biggie is Shamila's nickname for me. Something to do with my size. I don't think he means it unkindly. Lady Bunty, a pleasure to meet you. And who is this young lady?'

'Im Beatrice Ki–'

'Call her Bea,' Sammy cut in.

'Why do you have to re-name everybody, Shamila? It makes things so complicated!' Biggie raised his hands in frustration.

'Bea is actually better, thank you,' Bea chirped up in Sammy's defence, 'and it's simpler.'

'Okay, that's settled. Now, Shamila – sorry, Sammy – says you want to find some raptors, eh? You sure about that? Why not rest a day before heading into the jungle, go to the depot and get a permit?'

'Thank you, but we have already seen that brute at the depot and I would rather have nothing more to do with him,' said Bunty firmly.

'Christian Hayter? I presume then it's you two he's been asking around New Town for. He's cracking a few heads together trying to find out where you disappeared to and I find Sammy has already picked you up. Lucky for you. But he's not going to like you hunting on his island. No way.'

'Oh, we're not interested in hunting, Biggie. Quite the opposite,' said Bunty. 'We just want to see the raptors, you know, alive – singing and dancing. Surely we're allowed to look?'

'He does not like anything, Lady, I've seen him take a man down for the wrong look.'

Theodore stood up. 'Biggie, sir, we have travelled a long way to this island to find things and we want to see the raptors in their habitat, not in a cage. I can look after

Bunty and Bea, you just need to look after Junior and lead the way.'

'Don't forget me, Mr Hogan!' Sammy spoke up. 'Junior won't go without me.'

'We can pay what it costs,' Bunty chipped in.

'My fee is small . . .' began Biggie, before Sammy interrupted him with a cough and a very obvious elbow into his side. 'I mean, my fee will reflect market rates – but if Hayter finds out it may cost us more than just money.' He looked around the expectant group. 'Oh, go on then. I recognise a done deal when I see one. And you've already packed everything . . . including the chair? Shamila, you're in charge of explaining that one to your mother when we get back.'

6

Locket of Memories

~ almost invisible ~

Bea's new necklace was coming along very nicely. She was using one of Bunty's hatpins to make holes in the shells she had collected, then threading them along some fishing wire Theodore had produced from his kit bag (inside a tin marked 'Essentials'). Her guardians usually had a simple fix for most problems. Something that proved more complicated, though, was fixing Bea.

She had been barely two years old when her mother and father had left for a long trip to Australia. Bea had caught scarlet fever and it was too risky for her to travel – so her parents had left her with Bunty. They were only supposed to be gone for eight months, home in time for Christmas and Bea's third birthday. They never came home.

Bea only had photographs and her guardians' stories to remember her parents by; she was too young to have memories of her own. Theodore had practically grown up with Bea's mother, Grace, and his tales of their childhood together made it feel like Bea was right there with them. Bunty would fill in the finer details to Theodore's wild stories so that scents, sounds and images coloured the black-and-white photos and set them firmly in her granddaughter's imagination.

The most precious thing Bea owned was a silver locket on a long thin chain. It contained two small portraits of Grace and Franklin and was the last gift they had given their infant daughter. The shell necklace she was making would keep her parents in the locket around her neck company, let them know where their daughter was in the world. Bea continued boring small holes in the shells but Junior's swaying motion was making her feel a bit seasick. Theodore naturally had a fix for that – look up and out at the horizon, not down.

'Pocket, please,' Bea called out cheerfully. Theodore, walking alongside Junior, unbuckled his top right chest pocket and held it open for her to place the shells she was working on. Thanking him

with a smile earned her one of his charismatic winks in return. Bea knew that she was well looked after and cared for. Parents would be ideal, but Theodore and Bunty came a pretty awesome second place. Perhaps she was a bit ungrateful sometimes, she thought to herself.

In front of her, Sammy rode Junior's thick and heavily armoured neck with a long grey feather in one hand. Bea

sat cross-legged directly behind him on a rope saddle, with Bunty further behind, high up on the wicker chair, snoring gently.

Bea decided she'd rather walk for a while, to help with the motion sickness, and climbed down carefully to join Theodore.

Theodore was full of advice and information about all the different creatures they encountered. Junior was a fine example.

'Rule number one: never stand behind a kylos.'

This was good advice, as the saur's huge clubbed tail wagged happily, especially when he stopped to feast on juicy ferns. One blow could end their trek in a moment.

The flattened bony plates that covered Junior's back were ideal for piling up whatever had to be transported. Along both sides of his back the plates became more elongated and pointed, the very end ones protruding up and out like horns – ideal for tying things to. Sammy had made some improvements that Theodore had immediately noticed and admired.

To keep things from falling off Junior's back, grooves had been carved into the kylos's outer horns to secure the rope that weaved back and forth over the cargo, holding it all in place like a giant hair net.

Bea tapped Sammy on the shoulder. 'Why are you waving that long feather around over Junior's eyes?' Theodore looked around too, curious to hear the reason.

'Junior is a lot older than his name, and has very heavy eyelids,' Sammy replied and went on to explain further. 'You can tell his age not just by his long side spikes but also the thickness of the bony plates on his eyelids.'

'Okay, so he's old, with heavy eyelids. But why wave a feather in front of them?' Bea responded.

'Flies and bugs, simply. The jungle is full of them. He does not like to blink that often so I'm keeping them away for him. I help him, he helps me. I look after my staff, you know, feed him only the best ferns too.'

Theodore remembered the many porters whom he had used, who all whipped their kylos's lower necks to steer and keep their saurs in line. This boy had no need to dominate his kylos, just understand its needs and find a mutually beneficial arrangement.

'That's a new one on me as well, steering it like that,' Theodore said. 'Seen it done with elephants and brachiosaurs, but not with kylos.'

Bea looked down and to the side to see what Theodore was pointing at. Sammy was resting his feet on the bony neck spikes and had jammed each of his big toes behind Junior's earflaps. It looked like he was operating Junior's head with foot pedals.

Sammy furrowed his brow at Theodore. 'Does not everyone do this, Mr Slogan?'

'Nope, they would rather kick them than tickle them in the ear – people don't care too much for saurs of burden, my lad. And it's Logan by the way. Low-gan. Blimey,' he muttered.

Biggie had gone up ahead of them, checking that the path was clear. After a few hours the likelihood of being spotted by Hayter or his men had dropped – the jungle was getting thicker with every step. They caught up with Biggie as the narrow path opened up into a small clearing with a wooden shelter – just a roof really – that covered a stack of barrels and some long wooden crates. Biggie had swept the fallen leaves from the slightly raised platform under it and used them as kindling to start a fire in the pit next to it. He greeted them as Junior drew to a halt.

'Welcome, friends, to the Aru Rainforest Hotel! Our little holiday home away from the Old Town.'

'What is this place?' Bea asked Sammy.

'Not all the spice my father harvests goes to the depot for Hayter to take his cut – some sneaks off the island. Hayter does not have eyes everywhere.' He winked at Bea. 'The spice must flow.'

'We have one camp bed and a mosquito net for Lady

Bunty,' Biggie said, opening up the longest case and pulling out a canvas stretcher with fold-down legs. 'Sammy and I will string up some hammocks around the fire for the rest of us. Just because we're outdoors doesn't mean we can't be comfy.'

'Splendid,' said Bunty, genuinely surprised to find a little normality and comfort in the jungle.

'This is a proper bit of kit,' said Theodore, poking around in the case.

'Be careful there, Logan.' Biggie quickly moved a wooden case out of the way. 'Best I keep this out of the camp for tonight.'

Theodore tilted his head, read the stencilled 'EXPLOSIVES' sign and raised his eyebrows before looking more closely at a second box with relief.

'Army-issue medical gear as well?'

'Sure,' said Biggie. 'Can't take risks in the jungle.

Shadow raptors hide very well and can cut a man in two – and the poachers' traps are getting worse as well. I try to keep out of the war between them, but both sides are losing.'

'We heard something about shadow raptors earlier,' said Bunty, with a sideways look at Logan. 'Are they dangerous?'

'Well, they certainly can be. But then so can most things if you upset them. What did you think of Sammy's feather?' asked Biggie, as Sammy handed it to Bea. 'That's from a shadow raptor.'

'It's not the prettiest feather I've ever seen. The mottled grey colouring is a bit drab.'

'That's what makes them so special,' said Sammy. 'If it was brightly coloured Junior would be distracted by me waving it in front of him, but because it's drab, as you say, he barely notices it. The flies hate it, though.' Sammy took hold of Bea's hand that held the feather and shook it in front of her face back and forth.

'Oh yes, I see now – or rather I can't see it now, it's just a blur.' She waved it faster. 'Almost invisible, in fact!'

'Exactly. All the other raptors on and around these islands developed such colourful feathers, but this one species has done the opposite and made theirs blend into the shadows.'

'Successful camouflage,' said Bunty, listening in on Sammy's lesson. 'Is that why the shadow raptors are bigger than the other types of paradise raptors?'

'Yes and yes, Lady B. They were the number one predator before the hunters came. It's almost impossible to spot a shadow raptor with its cloak of camouflage blending it into the background. They are very good at stalking their prey – it's why they eat very well.' Sammy rubbed his tummy, 'And that is why they are bigger, like my papa.'

'Not just bigger, but much more intelligent,' added Biggie with a smile.

'Er, do they eat humans?' Bea couldn't help asking.

'There are many stories of people disappearing and shadow raptors are the first to take the blame. Where Raptors of Paradise are loud, colourful and stupid, the shadow raptors are quiet, cunning and clever.' Sammy tapped the side of his head, emphasising the point. 'The smaller, prettier species of raptors eat the many small rodents; the shadow raptors eat the larger mammals like the possum and tree kangaroo. Speaking of which, I had better get dinner on the fire. Sweet potato and fish stew!'

7

Eyes in the Jungle

~ Banji eggs for breakfast ~

The shadowy, feathered form was soundless as it drifted through the campsite. The humans were all in a deep sleep. It stopped at the nearest – a female – and watched for any movement. Something was different: its scent. With short, gentle sniffs the creature located the unusual smell surrounding her and inhaled deeply. The scent was unlike anything it had ever smelled before: fragrant like a flower but so intense it almost hurt. Unlike the other humans, this female slept on a strange raised nest, not in a cocoon. The creature lowered its head and looked under the nest. It found something worthy of a closer examination. Extending a claw, the creature gently pulled the object out and examined it before flipping it over a few times so that the contents fell onto the ground. Something heavy and shiny caught the moonlight; inside the container was a liquid, the source of the heady aroma. The creature dipped in for a good close sniff but the aroma was so powerful that it stung its small nose. It retracted its head quickly and gave three short sneezes.

Sammy, his rest momentarily disturbed, looked around but saw nothing and went back to sleep.

The dark shape of the creature had blended perfectly into the background. It stood stock still for a moment then moved silently past the human and a huge sleeping kylosaur and over to the other humans hanging in their cocoons. The one who hung the lowest was definitely the alpha male whose territory this was. His scent was everywhere – it clung to every object but he wasn't dangerous and he respected the paths of the jungle. The creature moved on. Stretching the whole length of the next cocoon lay another big male, perhaps a newcomer to the clan. This one had fur covering its mouth, and much paler skin.

What was interesting was the final cocoon. Due to its small size it must have a cub inside it; very rare to find one deep in the rainforest. There were traces of the pungent scent that the creature had picked up from the female, so this cub must belong to her. The cocoon completely covered its face so to get a better look the creature slowly pulled back the opening with a large claw, to reveal a mass of dark hair against a pale complexion. It was a female cub and it wore something that shone in the moonlight around its neck.

✦ ✦ ✦

'They're missing!' Bea's outburst woke the whole camp with a start. 'Mummy and Daddy are missing!' Bea then burst into tears as she had done on so many mornings in her life, awakening from her nightmare only for the horrible truth to sweep over her once more.

Theodore was the first to fall out of his hammock and comfort her, wrapping Bea up in his arms as she sat, sobbing, her head in her hands. 'There, there, it's okay, my love,' he said softly.

Bunty, meanwhile, was negotiating how to get out of the bed correctly without it overbalancing. She swung her legs round and as she placed them onto the ground noticed something under her foot. Her purse was on its side and everything had fallen out.

'Rats!' she muttered to herself, both as an explanation of the culprit and a curse in their name. 'I'm coming, Beatrice, just need some boots on.' She tapped them upside down as Theodore had shown her, to dislodge any unwelcome inhabitants, and took over from Theodore, who offered to make them all some tea.

'They're gone! Mummy and Daddy have disappeared off this island!' Bea wept and buried her head into Bunty's chest. 'They were here!'

'Don't be silly, my darling, it was just a dream,' soothed

— 73 —

Bunty, looking anxiously over Bea's head at Theodore, who had also heard Bea's comments and picked up on how close to the truth the girl was.

'No, it wasn't a dream,' said Bea, confused. 'My locket – it's gone! I had it last night and said goodnight to them, like every night, and now it's missing.'

'Oh, darling, I see. It must be here somewhere,' said Bunty, standing up and starting to hunt around. 'Maybe it just fell down a gap or something. Ask Sammy, every sort of rodent comes out at night. See, they've also had a good look over your shell necklace – the parts are scattered about over here.'

Bunty bent down and started to pick the shells up while Bea began to get herself under control. Her shoulders still shaking, she drew in a few breaths. 'Sorry, everybody,' she whispered.

'No need to be sorry. We'll clear this up and find your locket,' said Bunty bracingly. 'Look over at my bed, the rascals have been through my bag as well and spilt my perfume!'

Over by the campfire, Sammy had boiled up the kettle for hot drinks. Theodore held out the cups and Sammy poured the tea.

'Is Bea okay?' he asked worriedly. 'Your poor daughter.'

'I'm not her father, just her godfather,' Theodore replied quietly. 'She lost her parents long ago. They were good friends of mine. The best. Poor Bea still has nightmares.'

'I'm sorry to hear that,' said Sammy with a sad look in his eyes.

Biggie stepped back into the clearing, balancing his hat upside down in one hand.

'Think we had more than rats last night.' He spoke loudly enough for everyone to hear, and produced a short, mottled, grey feather from his pocket, which he gave to Bea. 'Raptors as well. This wasn't here yesterday evening.'

'Shadow raptor?'

'Yes, I think this is a forelimb feather.' Biggie smiled at Bea as she tucked it in her hair. 'Now I've also found breakfast – fresh eggs. Who's hungry?' In his hat were three large speckled eggs, each about the size of a grapefruit.

'What kind of jungle fowl laid those?' asked Bunty.

'These are not bird eggs, they are from a banji. We have them all over the island; it's a type of oviraptor,' Biggie explained. 'Ugly-looking and worse to roast, very tough tasteless meat, but their eggs are

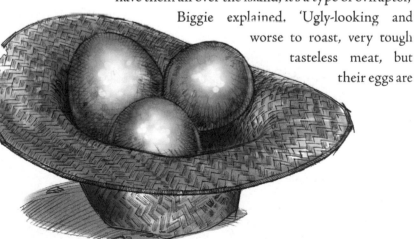

delicious.'

Banji eggs for breakfast in the soft morning light was more than enough to lift everyone's spirits, but as the others packed and got ready to keep moving, Bea was still on her hands and knees going over every inch of the jungle floor. Her locket was still missing. There seemed to be a few shells missing, too, but they were probably still in Theodore's pockets. However calm she tried to be, she felt awful at losing such a precious thing; the last thing her parents had given her. Sammy came over to help and for a while they silently scoured the area below where her hammock had been strung.

'Can shadow raptors steal things?' she pondered out loud.

'Yes,' said Sammy simply.

'You mean one came in and took the locket from around my neck?' She reached for it instinctively, but her hand came away empty.

'No,' Sammy replied.

Bea scrunched her face in frustration. 'Yes and no?'

'A shadow raptor has claws not fingers – it could not have taken the locket from your neck without you noticing. It was probably the winged spirits.'

'Spirits! What do you mean?'

'The spirits of the people who have disappeared in the jungle. People have seen them; they have angel wings.'

Bunty, who was pretending not to listen, looked over to Theodore.

'It's true,' said Biggie. 'I've had money stolen, grain sacks, sometimes tools and rope – lots of rope.'

'What does a spirit want with money?' Bea asked.

'They like shiny things, I guess,' Sammy replied.

'Don't be so silly,' Bunty said sharply. 'Beatrice, take no notice. They are teasing you.'

Sammy looked over to his father who shrugged and changed the subject quickly.

'Shall we all have one more look for the locket together? After that, Bea, I'm sorry but we really will have to get moving.'

Theodore decided an incentive might help lighten the mood. 'Great idea, Biggie, we'll give it another go. Keep your eyes peeled, campers. First person to see it gets ten quid.'

✦ ✦ ✦

For the feathered creature, high up in the tree above, the politics of the situation were all wrong. The female cub was demanding a lot of attention and everyone including the alpha male was helping her do something. Her cry of distress had startled everything in the area and the creature was puzzled. As the humans moved around the base of the tree the creature followed them silently, carefully manoeuvring one foot in front of the other above them to get a better view through the thick leaves.

An ankle feather became dislodged on a branch of the tree and fluttered down into the clearing, landing softly just behind the cub. Its loose feathers should have been plucked out yesterday but there had been no space or time to do this whilst stalking the humans . . .

✦ ✦ ✦

Below, Bea turned and saw that she must have dropped her feather, so picked it up to stick it back into her hair but found that it was still there. So this was a new feather – but where had it come from? She looked up, puzzled. And there, staring straight back at her, were two cold blue eyes. Frozen in the moment Bea went to open her mouth but it had suddenly dried up in fear. She extended her arm and tapped Theodore on the back.

'I'm sorry, Bea, it's just not here,' he huffed.

She tapped again with a lot more force, then turned and grabbed his arm. Theodore swung around, 'Yes?' He saw the colour was drained from her face. 'Bea, love, what's happened? You okay?'

Still unable to talk, she turned and pointed up.

'What's up there?' Theodore followed the direction of her finger.

'Eyes in the trees,' she croaked.

'Where?' Theodore looked about.

'They were up, up here . . .' She blinked hard and swallowed. 'The raptor was up there.'

'You sure?' Theodore held her shoulder. 'It was

probably a tree kangaroo.'

'Its eyes were looking straight at me!' Bea shivered out the words.

'You could hide a bus up there, the canopy is so thick. Whatever it is, it'll be more scared of us than we are of it, trust me. Come on, let's get out of here.'

* * *

The creature pondered the situation. Was it the shiny cold shell that they were looking for? Why had it caused so much distress? The creature delved deep under its forelimb feathers and pulled out a tight bundle of matted twigs and moss that looked like it was once a small bird's nest. From this, it gently untangled Bea's locket.

Taking one last glance at the faces within, it held out its small finger and covered each of their heads. They were exactly the same size as its fingertips. Snapping the silver casing shut, it paused for a second, then lowered its arm and gently dropped the locket into the bush where the boy cub was searching.

* * *

Sammy suddenly leapt up in the air.

'Woo-hoo! I've found it!' He handed Bea her silver locket. 'Mr Thesaurus, you owe me big bucks!'

8

The Lucky Rhiptus Rhat

~ *the Blue Horned Raptor of Paradise* ~

Bunty settled into her seat on top of Junior, turning away to give the men privacy to put the fire out one by one. Bea got comfortable in Sammy's saddle and turned to see what was taking so long. As soon as she realised how they were putting out the fire she turned back quickly and blushed. She also needed to relieve herself, but decided to wait to find somewhere more private to answer nature's call.

The mood was upbeat as Theodore led the way, hacking at the occasional branch that obscured the pathway, whistling a joyful tune. Biggie followed, occasionally stopping and holding his hand to his ear, only to wave everybody on again. Sammy led Junior on his lead, leaving Bea to have a go steering and wafting the long shadow raptor feather in front of the kylos's face. After a while the calm was accompanied by gentle snoring that drifted down from Bunty's high perch. From above the path looked inviting but, judging by the more frequent hacking of Theodore's machete and Biggie's mutterings under his breath, the going was starting to get tough.

Above, the treetops constantly thrashed with the activity and calls of unseen creatures but Bea did not look up. Just the thought of seeing those eyes staring back at her sent a cold shudder down her spine. Suddenly the chair strapped to Junior's back shook violently and Bunty started to panic.

'Stop! Stop! Help!'

Bea quickly did as Sammy had shown her and applied both toes forcefully into Junior's ears, halting him instantly.

'Try not to wave your arms about! I will climb up and get it off you!' Sammy called up.

'What is it? What's happening?' By now Bea had squeezed her eyes shut. She could not bear to look. What was attacking Bunty?

'Hold still, Bunty, Sammy can help,' Biggie said. 'Very lucky, very lucky, it's lunch time!'

Whose lunch? Bea thought. Biggie was laughing hard and this did not help.

Sammy sprinted up past Bea to Bunty, who was not doing as she was told and was waving her arms about frantically.

'I think it's time you travelled down here with us in second class,' Biggie joked as he held out his hand to help Bunty down to the ground. Bea opened her eyes and looked around to see her grandmother with her hair all over the place and Sammy untangling the foot of a very large, flapping rhiptus rhat.

'That was not a nice way to wake up, I can assure you,' Bunty said, accepting Biggie's hand.

'Come now, around here it's lucky to catch a rhat and this is a fine one.' Biggie grinned. 'I will get a fire on and toast it for us to share.'

Bunty looked him squarely in the eyes. 'Mr Biggie, I'm finding your humour hard to join in with. I will *not* be eating that ghastly creature.'

Sammy had quickly despatched the poor rhat and now its oversized head with toothy, beaked snout lolled about under one of its paper-thin brightly iridescent wings. 'Look, Bea, it's a beauty.' Sammy held it out for her to inspect.

Indeed it was more attractive than the smaller common brownish rhamp rhats in her grandmother's barn that flew out at dusk and caught flies on the wing during warm summer evenings. 'You eat them?' she asked.

'Sure, not out of choice but we don't want to waste a meal in the jungle. Every living thing has to eat, so something has to be lunch.'

✦ ✦ ✦

Bunty was as good as her word and would not try the rhiptus rhat, instead satisfying herself with a papaya. Bea gave it a go, though, and once she had brushed off the charred fine hair with a stick, found that the white tender meat inside was just like roast chicken. Theodore went in for a wing, but Bea could see that he was only pretending to enjoy the burnt fingers. 'Try the tail!' Sammy offered but she declined. The bony foot-long stump looked like it offered nothing juicy.

'Tell me, Biggie,' Bunty said, wiping her chin on the sleeve of her thorn-proof safari suit that was today's chosen outfit. 'These raptors, when might we possibly see them?'

'You may not see them, lady. They don't like company and as I have said, we have to be very quiet.'

Bea had been putting it off since they left camp but there was no way to hold it back any longer – she needed to empty her bladder. Wiping the remaining flecks of burnt rhat skin off her hands she stood, excused herself and wandered behind a tree . . . and straight into another rhiptus that was hanging from a low branch. It screeched louder then her and within seconds Sammy was wafting it away. 'Double lucky! You okay, Busy Bee?'

'Fine, not fine . . . can you stand guard for me, Sammy?' Bea couldn't help blushing. 'I need to relieve myself,' she whispered.

'Okay, sure, but I would not do it here – look, red ants!' He pointed to the ground that was alive and starting to engulf her shoes.

Sammy led Bea past a fallen tree and over to a series of moss-covered boulders that formed a secluded haven, perfect for Bea to do her business. 'I'll stand here and won't peek, I promise.'

Knowing Sammy was watching out for her, Bea quietly answered nature's call. Relieved, she straightened up and noticed something that stood out against the mix of greens that made up the jungle floor. A white shell. She stepped over to it and looked closer.

A white shell with a tiny hole drilled in the base, made for a necklace.

'Sammy, take a look at this?'

'No, no, Bea. I'm standing here not looking!'

'I'm finished, Sammy, you can come – look!' She pointed at the shell.

Sammy turned around and immediately dropped to the floor.

'Get down!' he hissed.

Bea, puzzled, joined Sammy as he held his finger up to his lips and pointed through the ferns.

Bea followed his finger and there, hopping towards them, was the most extraordinary Raptor of Paradise, lighting up the otherwise uniformly green surroundings.

At first sight it looked like an oversized pheasant or cockerel but this was no ordinary jungle fowl. It had a feathered head of deep red with a vivid pale blue muzzle and large comical white circles around its black eyes, making it look like it had just stepped out of a cartoon. Its golden-orange body was supported by strong black legs with stubby red-tipped ankle-feathers.

Mesmerised, they watched as the raptor hopped about, tilting its head, checking if it had company. Thinking it was alone, the raptor proceeded to pick up in its muzzle the twigs and leaves that were scattered on the floor, tossing them aside. A larger branch had fallen across its path and had to be kicked violently away. Its arena cleared, it was time to redecorate. It was not until the raptor leapt into the air that Bea and Sammy noticed the delicate blossoming of pale blue flowers high in the canopy above the clearing. Catching a stem in its mouth, the raptor pulled a bloom to the ground and gently plucked off the petals one by one, discarding what it did not require. The tiny petals were too small to manoeuvre with its claws or teeth but that did not stop the raptor arranging them in a perfect ring. It lowered its head and exhaled with enough force to scatter the petals just the right distance away, forming a larger circle. One or two petals needed their place perfecting, but otherwise it had managed the task effortlessly.

Sammy nudged Bea and pointed at the mossy boulders that surrounded them. A very plain-looking raptor was standing on a boulder; the female shared only one characteristic to the beautiful male raptor below – its comical, goggly eyes.

The male raptor also noticed its audience and shyly jumped behind a rock that Bea saw had been cleaned of all moss – this had to be part of its performance. A quiet moment passed and Sammy nudged Bea again, knowing something spectacular was about to happen, and it did.

The male raptor jumped confidently back out into the centre of the blue ring of petals with a renewed swagger and proceeded to gulp in air from its wide open mouth. Suddenly two bright blue fleshy horns parted the red feathers on its head and grew upwards. It shook its head a few times, helping to erect them and also unveiling a wattle of loose blue skin from under its chin. Unlike the soft red wattles of flesh around a chicken's face, the raptor's wattle unravelled downwards over its entire front and then filled out across its chest with a striking pattern of bright red, violet and blue. In moments it had transformed into the strangest-looking raptor Bea had ever seen.

Then, with all its might, it let out a long chorus of deep nasal tones, much like a bagpiper. As it did so it jutted its head to the left and right, flapping its large bright wattle. The sound resonated around them and filled the jungle. Bea's eyes sparkled; this truly was a spectacle.

However, the female was looking less than impressed and kept twitching its head away from the display. Undeterred, the male puffed out again and stood bolt upright, then moved towards its potential mate with a 'come and get it' strut. But it only got halfway before the female had had enough. It darted off behind the boulder and disappeared.

The male raptor hopped up onto the rock where the female had been, looked down on the arena and spotted what had distracted the female. It quickly darted back down to the floor, picked up the tiny white shell in its muzzle and tossed it away. One last check to confirm that the female was definitely gone and it darted off into the undergrowth, leaving its arena for nature to reclaim. Falling leaves were already beginning to gather in the clearing.

'Wow!' Sammy turned to Bea, who was still mesmerised. 'Told you that rhiptus would bring you great luck. That was the Blue Horned Raptor of Paradise, or as we call it a Bluepan – super-super rare.'

Bea stood up with difficulty, her knees locked from being so still in one position. 'Did you see what it did with the shell?'

'The white one?'

Bea stepped over and picked it up between her fingers to inspect it – 'Yes, that's my shell,' – and placed it in Sammy's open palm. 'It has the hole that I made in it for the necklace, the one I'm making.'

'Mmm. The Bluepan did not like it distracting his female. Too bad after all the hours he spent cleaning his dance arena, decorating it with the petals, refining his plumage, practising his dance . . . all spoilt by just one little white shell.' He handed it back to Bea. 'Tomorrow might be his day. Why did you put it there?' he asked.

'I didn't, Sammy. I was over there, finishing my business when I saw it, that was what I wanted to show you, but you saw the raptor first.'

'Come on, you must have dropped it.'

'No, honestly, Sammy, I didn't drop it. How could it have got over there?'

But Sammy was more excited about the raptor than the mystery of the shell and wanted to get back to tell the others, so she reluctantly let the subject drop.

The others were at first sceptical of the raptor sighting but Sammy led them back to the arena and Biggie confirmed it to be genuine. Bunty uncovered a pile of discarded petals, probably from the previous day, that had been neatly brushed away and one of the Bluepan's old tail feathers, which pleased her greatly. 'At last! Something to take home.'

Theodore pulled out his notebook and jotted down some particulars. 'Bea, you're better than me – can you sketch the scene for me while it's fresh in your mind, show what the little fellow looked like?'

Bea wanted to move on – the shell had unnerved her – but she got out her notebook and watercolours and obliged as best she could. It was an hour before they finally moved on, leaving the secluded sanctuary as they had found it.

◆ ◆ ◆

A mile away, back at the morning's campsite, the fire had not completely gone out. A log was still smouldering and the pungent smoke had drifted through the thick undergrowth, giving away its location. One of Hayter's men kicked the log to one side and leant in close to inspect it.

'We got company, Bishop.'

Bishop, now wearing a comical turban of bandages, dismounted his mule.

'What kind, Ash?'

'This is where my acute tracking skills come in handy . . .' Ash looked around at the trodden ground and broken leaves.

'Two heavy-footed, two light-footed and . . .' He prodded his finger into a curious-looking mark dotted all over the ground. 'Funny, not seen that before . . . slender and smaller-pointed shoes, ladies' shoes.'

Bishop widened his eyes. 'We should go back and tell the boss.'

'By the time he gets here the tracks will be washed away after the next downpour of rain.'

Bishop scrunched his face in thought.

'Why don't I go back and get him while you go on ahead, track them with your skilled nose and find out where they are and what they are up to?'

Ash looked up. 'Don't be silly, mate; I can't smell them. I taste the air, the ground . . . I feel their presence . . .' He lifted up some of the ash that had turned to a yellowish white clay, looked at it and dipped his tongue in, pretending to get some divine inspiration from it to impress his less-than-clever friend. But instead he instantly spat it out and wiped his cuff over his lips.

'Ammonia!' he muttered, trying to play down the situation and look cool as the acrid taste contorted his face.

9

The Teddy Bear's Picnic

~ *seeing stars* ~

In the afternoon everyone was keen to be the next to spot a raptor. Bunty had sat behind Sammy riding Junior, but found it less than comfortable so opted to 'take an afternoon walk'. Bea helped as best she could to untangle her grandmother as Bunty attracted every branch, vine and creeper to herself like a magnet, but she was not put off – 'It might be hot, but it's certainly no more prickly than the brambles where I grew up,' – so Bea left Bunty to struggle on and went ahead to help Theodore.

'Theo.'

'Bea?'

'Pocket, please!' She held out her necklace shell that she had found with Sammy in the clearing. She had been clutching it for the last few hours and pondering.

'Certainly, but what's up?' Theodore looked carefully at Bea, judging she had something on her mind.

'I know you'll think I'm crazy, but . . . but I think we're being followed.'

Theodore turned around and looked behind them.

'You're right, but they're not hiding very well . . . ' He gestured back to the others who were unstrapping the chair that was sitting too high on Junior's back to pass under the trees this deep into the jungle.

Bea huffed.

'Seriously, Bea, I believe you saw something, just not what your imagination is letting you believe it to be. Look above us.' Theodore lifted her chin and they both gazed up at the dancing light that streaked down through the foliage in thin shards. The air was alive with the hum of insects and birds constantly chattering. 'There are a million eyes looking back at us because we are strangers in this environment. We probably look very silly to them.'

As ever, Theodore had a way and the words to ease the situation.

'Your mother would be so proud to know that her girl can muck in with anyone . . . and even find the elusive Raptors of Paradise! You're doing great, girl – chin up.' He mocked a punch that landed softly on her chin and smiled down on her proudly. 'Now, will you be okay here while I get that blasted chair down and strap Bunty safely to that poor painted beast so she keeps out of trouble?'

Bea grinned as Theodore winked and made his way back with a whistle.

The jungle canopy occasionally opened up where trees had fallen, allowing light to bathe the ground and sending up a mist of sparkles in the moist air. Ahead of Bea was such a scene. Vaulting the long tree trunk that had created this oasis of light, Bea landed in a pool of freshly exposed undergrowth and immediately noticed that some other creatures had sought sanctuary here. The sight was quite surreal: four large red tree kangaroos looked around at her, wide-eyed, just like a fanciful illustration from a children's book of a teddy bears' picnic in the woods. As soon as Bea stopped and smiled, three of them bolted, each heading for a tree to scamper up. Their agility was impressive and soon they were well out of sight high above her. Returning her eyes to the ground she noticed the fourth was still there, watching her with its deep black eyes. She paused, wondering why it had not followed the others and edged slowly towards it, half a foot at a time, but it just looked at her and didn't move. 'You poor thing, the others have left you alone.' She thought it best to calmly befriend the sweet velvet creature. 'Don't be scared now, it's just little old Bea.' Her confidence grew the closer she got.

A few steps closer revealed all. The tree kangaroo was attached to a log by a short length of wire around its neck. 'Why would anyone want to do that to a lovable furball like you?' She moved to help it, but, before she could, something appeared at lightning speed by her side. A feathered creature grabbed her, and hard.

Within seconds Bea was flying through the air, landing on her back with a thud a good few feet away, with the creature on top of her. Winded by the speed and force of

the landing she tried to focus her vision to make sense of what was going on. She could feel feathers in her fingers and there was a silhouetted head above her with a halo of dazzling shimmering light around it. *Is this an angel? Am I dead?* she thought, the pressure on her lungs making her unable to breathe. She felt extremely light-headed. Then suddenly the weight on her lifted and as air filled her lungs things came a little more into focus. Stars fluttered in the light that surrounded the figure, and she saw it was not an angel. Those cold, blue, dangerous-looking eyes stared down at her. Flooded with fear and desperately trying to catch her breath, Bea choked. The figure moved, letting the full force of sunlight hit her in the face, sending Bea's already blurred vision out of focus once more. It took a while for her eyes to adjust and as they did so she realised she was not seeing stars, but leaves sent high into the air that were now finding their way back to the ground around her.

The figure had gone.

Back down the track, the thud of Bea's landing had been heard by Theodore, who quickly turned, dropping the kit he was holding to scramble up the path towards her. The illuminated clearing he had noticed before now had a new feature. In the centre, suspended up high, was a large net with something big in it desperately scrabbling to get out.

'Bea! Bea, stay still! I'll get you down!' he frantically called out, taking the fallen tree in one leap and trying to judge what exactly this contraption was before sighting a rope that was somehow supporting it. He dashed over and drew out his knife, grabbing the upper part of the rope before slashing it in two below his supporting hands. The tension on the rope was greater than he had imagined, and releasing it jerked him up in the air like a counterbalance as the net slackened off and unfolded on one side.

'Bea, I've got you!' Theodore called out, even though he was now the one dangling a few feet up in the air. As the net continued to unravel something snapped under his weight, sending him crashing down to the ground. He rolled over and quickly tried to find an opening in the tangled net. Finding what looked like an edge he shot under it, grabbing Bea in his arms and lifting her from the ground – only to find not Bea, but a red tree kangaroo with a very startled look on its face.

'She's here, Mr Shogun!' Sammy called out as he and Biggie, who had just caught up, did a double-take seeing the cuddly creature in Theodore's arms. He let go and in a flash the tree kangaroo shot up the closest tree, following its friends with a joyful *whoop-whoop*.

Sammy had found Bea a few yards away, stiff with shock and not able to talk but in one piece.

'Just you rest there.' Bunty rushed to her granddaughter, propping her up and cradling her head. 'Biggie, what is this horrid device?'

'This, my lady, is the worst kind of trap, not for catching but for killing.'

As he sheathed his knife and patted himself down, Theodore looked up at Biggie and nodded.

'Yes, it's quite an elaborate contraption. Looks like the bait – the tree kangaroo, in this case – is pulled away in a net, to be saved for another day. And judging by the tension on this rope, the victim would have snapped its neck as it's hoisted into the air and cracked like a whip!'

'You were so lucky you were not harmed, Beatrice.' Bunty continued to comfort her granddaughter but Bea knew that it was not luck that had saved her. Somehow the creature or spirit with the dangerous eyes had.

'Who on earth would be doing this?' Bunty asked but she had a good idea of who that person was.

Biggie sighed. 'Your friend Christian Hayter – his misery has no limits. This trap had a tree kangaroo as bait;

that's too big for the smaller Raptors of Paradise.'

'So this is for shadow raptors, correct?' Theodore asked.

'What else? They are the biggest natural predators on the island and Hayter's personal battles against them go back a long time. He wants to be the top predator and he is sadly winning the war.'

'Aren't all the raptors here in trouble?'

'Yes, this island once teemed with them but now, as you know, they are very scarce. The good-looking colourful ones have a value, their feathers fetch a good price, but the shadow raptors, their feathers are worthless, so Hayter kills them just for fun.'

'And for feeding to his pet tyrant,' Bunty chipped in.

'The Beast is not a pet. It's . . . a monster. It has no place on this island. Its presence is to bring fear to everything, including to us humans. The last person to stand up to Hayter was . . . eaten.'

Bunty's lips narrowed and her face filled with anger.

'This, I am afraid, is as far as we can go,' Biggie said firmly.

'But we have not met the Raptors of Paradise yet.' Theodore stood tall. 'Or at least only Bea and Sammy have. Bunty and I wish to see them too.'

'Look here,' Biggie said, 'many people go looking in this jungle and now you know why they don't always return. Hayter has brought death to this island – you must return with us before he realises you have come into his jungle and now that you have broken this trap. This is not good for his business and you will pay. Trust me, you will pay with your lives.'

'I'm not afraid of him.' Theodore squared himself up.

'Me neither.' Bunty backed him up.

'Well, I am,' said Biggie. 'Sammy and I are leaving. If you are crazy enough to stay, then good luck. I can't afford to get mixed up in this sort of fight.' Biggie rested his hands on his son's shoulders. 'It's all very well for you, you can get on a boat and leave, but we have to live with the consequences of what we do, and I must protect my family.'

Bunty said nothing but systematically broke every part of Hayter's elaborate trap as Biggie and Sammy made preparations to leave.

10

The Rainbow Eucalyptus Tree

~ page 134 ~

Although Biggie's mind was made up to leave with Sammy, somehow Bunty negotiated for Junior to stay, as he was loaded with all the kit and there was no way they could continue without him. Biggie just took some water and his small pack of belongings. Sammy was worried about Bea. 'You look after Junior, Busy Bee,

EUCALYPTUS DEGLUPTA

Commonly known as the Rainbow eucalyptus, Mindanao gum, Rainbow gum.

This tree can grow up to 6 ft wide and over 200 ft tall and thrives in tropical forests.

It is found growing naturally in an area that spans New Britain, New Guinea, Sulawesi and Mindanao, and is the only Eucalyptus species with a natural range that extends into the northern hemisphere.

The unique multi-coloured bark is the most distinctive feature of the tree. Patches of outer bark are shed annually at different times, showing a bright green inner bark. This then darkens and matures to give blue, purple, orange and then maroon tones. The previous season's bark below is off in strips to reveal a brightly coloured new bark below. The peeling process results in vertical streaks of red, orange, green, blue and gray. The colours of the bark are not as intense outside the tree's native range.

The tree is one of the fastest known growing trees in the world therefore it is widely cultivated around the world in tree plantations, mainly for pulpwood that is used in making white paper. The biggest pulpwood plantations are situated in the Philippines.

It is also used cultivated as an ornamental tree, for planting in tropical and subtropical gardens and parks. In the U.S.A. rainbow eucalyptus grows in the frost-free climates found in Hawaii and the southern portions of California, Texas and Florida but only grows to heights of 100 to 125 feet, only about half the height it can reach in its native range.

134

Mature Tree

Flower

Leaf Structure

Young Tree

Bark

and he will look after you, remember that.'

The previous day's events and the following sleepless night had consumed everyone's energy. No one had the strength to speak, instead reliving and thinking over what had happened, each coming to the conclusion that perhaps they ought not to be heading deeper into the jungle, especially without Biggie and Sammy. But, each too proud to admit defeat or their own shortcomings, they trudged on, only stopping when Junior decided to eat or relieve himself. Bea in particular had much on her mind. She had been scared by her narrow miss with the trap and couldn't stop thinking about it – and her mysterious saviour.

Eventually Theodore stopped and turned to Bea and Bunty.

'Let's call it a day here – this tree looks like it can offer us better shelter from the rain that . . .' He looked up as the sky darkened and rain lashed the top of the jungle canopy.

Bea shivered and retreated close to the brightly coloured tree trunk. Bunty removed her long coat and placed it over Bea's shoulders. 'Here you are, darling, this will keep the rain off.'

'What kind of tree is this?' Bea asked Theodore as he tethered Junior and quickly unstrapped their essential kit from the kylos.

'Ask me any other question, just not about trees – not my speciality.'

Bea looked curiously upwards. The tree had grown over a large rock and was supported by deep buttress roots that wrapped around it and spanned outwards. Its branches were low and wide and from them hung a fine vine that created a sanctuary from the otherwise repetitive rainforest canopy outside. The foliage hanging down reminded Bea of a willow tree, but each shard of this tree's peeling bark revealed a different vivid colour of the rainbow. The layers of red, orange, yellow, green, blue, indigo and violet resembled crude brushstrokes on a child's painting. Bea lifted off a section, examining the bark closely before placing it in her own bag of essentials.

'This was one of your father's field guides – look, *Trees of the Tropics*,' Bunty said as she took out a well-worn book from one of her cases that was still strapped to Junior. 'What do you think the tree is called?'

'I don't know.' Bea patted the trunk and pondered. 'A rainbow tree?'

Bunty opened up the book and ran her finger up and down the index until she stopped and tapped the page. 'Page 134.' Leafing back through large sections, she glanced over at Bea and smiled. 'Correct. The Rainbow Eucalyptus Tree, or *Eucalyptus deglupta*, to be precise.'

Bea looked up. 'Seriously?'

Bunty handed her the open book, the page starting to get spotted with rain.

'Here, take my umbrella. Sit down, have a read.'

Bea took her grandmother's advice and sat on one of the raised buttress roots that span out from the base of the tree and angled the umbrella so that it was completely covering her. For a short while she could remove herself from the horrid wet jungle and focus on something that was not putting one foot in front of the other.

Page 134 revealed a colourful description that matched the magnificent tree in front of her very well. Sadly Bea's enthusiasm did not stretch to learning about the Red Flowering Eucalyptus Tree on the next page so she closed the book. However, something else in its pages was of interest. Bea paused for a moment, then opened the cover to look at the very first page. *Franklin Kingsley, 1908* was written inside. Bea thought with some comfort that, even here, her beloved father was close by. She shut the book again and put it into one of the deep pockets of Bunty's coat round her shoulders.

As she did so, her hand brushed something else. She pulled it out. It was the familiar sight of her mother's letters, addressed to Bea and bound together with a red cord. Bunty always kept them safely with her and often read them aloud to Bea to keep her mother's memory alive. But something was different about the top envelope. Bea slid it out from the others and compared it to the one below. It was less well thumbed, it had not faded and there were an array of different stamps on it. And Bea had never seen it before.

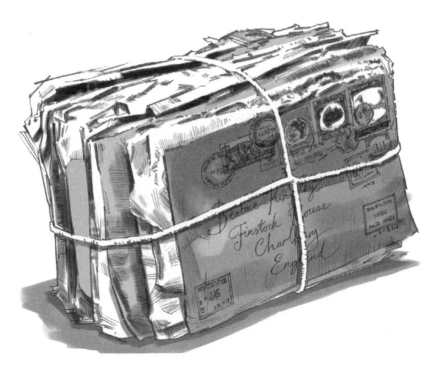

Koto Baru
Wokan, Aru Islands
Maluku Province
Eastern Indonesia

Dear Beatrice,

As you will see from the lovely stamps and postmark we have finally left Australia and are making the long trip back around the world to be home with you in about a month's time.

After a bumpy crossing we have arrived on the Islands of Aru, just south of Papua. Franklin wanted to stop here to take a shore excursion into the rainforest, where we hope to see some of the amazing Raptors of Paradise. Whilst in Darwin we saw some Birds of Paradise that have colourful plumes and we have been told the raptors are even more delightful, with strange dances and a unique chorus. Your father claims it to be for serious research purposes but I know he is just as excited as I am to see them in the wild. The colourful feather enclosed has just been given to me by a lovely local woman we are boarding with, but I promise to *acquire some more for you on our return.*

For reasons too long and complicated to describe here, the last few days have been the most exhausting and enjoyable ever, and your father and I can't wait to be home with you soon to share with everyone a big surprise. It will be the best present to return with and one I know you will love and look after forever.

Always and forever, your loving mother,
Grace xxx

The words trembled on the page with every tear.

Blinking her blurred wet eyes, Bea looked again at the envelope and saw a pencilled note next to the line of stamps. It read: *Sorry for the delay!*

Bea held the letter close to her nose and inhaled, but nothing struck a chord except a distant aroma of ginger. She reread its sweet and intoxicatingly vivid words but came back to the same confused conclusion. It was now crystal-clear the real reason why they had come to this remote island. But why had her grandmother and Theodore kept this letter a secret? Did they think she was too young or too easily scared to know the truth?

Bea lifted the umbrella that was sheltering her and peered out at Bunty and Theodore, who were making a shelter and starting a fire.

'I'm thirteen years OLD,' she muttered to herself, 'not YOUNG.'

The flickering of the campfire made the shadows around the campsite dance with joy. However, the mood within the camp was quite different. Bea was distracted in her thoughts. Even the ever-present thundering of insects and the occasional screeching of some poor and unfortunate unknown creatures deep in the jungle could not take her mind off her mother's letter. Bea had returned the book and Bunty's coat without her grandmother realising she had read the new letter. She wanted to say something but the time was not right. Best to wait and see what was going on as clearly they were not here in the Islands of Aru to just see the Raptors of Paradise. It was now obvious why, only two days after the end of summer term, they were en route here without any forward planning. Bunty must have received the letter and set off straight away. Were they really expecting Bea's parents to be here at the dock waiting as the boat came in? Her grandmother's need to visit the post office as soon as they got off the boat was now easily explained – but what had Bunty and Theodore learnt there?

Bea was trying to pluck up the courage to guide the evening's conversation in this direction, to ask out loud, *Do you think Mummy and Daddy ever came here?* but deep down she did not want to know the answer, or the truth. After eleven long and painful years Bea knew the only news would be bad news.

Bea could see that Theodore had something on his mind as well. He was busy unpacking his army sack, lining up its contents on his groundsheet, inspecting everything with his trusty eye and, for some unknown reason, blowing on things as if a thin layer of dust had settled on there in the time between cleaning and re-cleaning. Bea knew this routine well: it meant that Theo was avoiding a conversation. Bunty was doing the equivalent. Her handbag, more like a hand-sack, contained everything most valuable to her and she too was trying to find something by tipping out its contents, looking deep into an empty bag and then replacing everything item by item, in order of importance. The bundle of her daughter's letters were not there and it would have been a good moment for Bea to casually mention in passing that they were in her coat pocket . . . but before the words and courage formed, Bunty spoke.

'Where are they?'

'Where's who?' Theodore answered.

Bunty turned, met Theodore's eyes and spoke her mind firmly.

'Grace and Franklin. Where are they, Theodore? What on earth are we doing out here in this horrible jungle?'

Bea stared as her grandmother held her hands up to her head and sobbed.

Theodore stood quickly and plucked his handkerchief from the kit in front of him and held it out to Bunty. 'Here.' Theodore looked over to Bea, who was still staring. 'Come now, we're all tired; compose yourself, Bunty.'

Bea had not considered how Bunty would be feeling about the new letter. And suddenly, here was her grandmother asking the very same question that she wanted, or did not want, the answer to. Bea and Bunty were two generations apart, separated by Grace, whom they both loved and missed deeply. Bea leapt up out of her hammock and ran over to Bunty. She wrapped her arms around her and they fell into each other.

'Grandma, please stop asking questions that have no answer!'

'Darling, I'm so sorry. I feel that I have not been truthful with you.'

Bea took a breath. 'Don't fret, Grandma. I've read the letter and I know why we are here.'

Bunty held on tighter. 'So you know this may be where they spent their last days? I am so sorry, Bea, but I had to find out what brought them here.'

'We've all wished that one day they would return, but I think now I know that the real truth is they won't.'

'I believe you're right, Beatrice. I have been treating you as a child for too long. You're smarter than I give you credit for.'

Bea blushed and wiped the tears from her eyes.

'I'd hoped to find answers or clues, at least,' Bunty continued, 'but we must be realistic. Maybe we will never find out what happened. Let's all pray that coming here can bring us some closure to this terrible matter.'

Theodore, towering over them both, held his arms wide, bent down and embraced them. He did not need to say anything: his strength had boundaries, but his heart had none.

After a while, he pulled away a little and said, 'In the army it got tough, tougher than I can ever say, but what you both have had to deal with is the worst sort of pain that anyone can endure. The loss of a truly loved one: of a child, of parents. Let's not fight each other but help fix each other.'

Bunty and Bea sobbed in agreement into his chest.

'It's night,' Theodore went on. 'Nothing can happen now. Tomorrow let's head back to see Biggie and Sammy and get off this rock. Another thing I learnt in the army was never to kick a hornet's nest – the smallest things hurt the most. We have made enemies here on an island with no laws to protect us. Both of you need to promise me that you will follow my lead and I will get you home safely.'

Sobbing in unison, Bea and Bunty both promised. They hugged for a while longer before Theodore adopted a more stern tone.

'Right. We're moving out at dawn, lights out in five minutes. I will take the first watch. If you need to *relieve yourselves*, you need to do it *swiftly*. MOVE IT!'

It was not long before Bunty and Bea were asleep and adding their snores to the myriad of noises created by the other critters around them.

◆ ◆ ◆

The grass at home was long, longer than usual. *It must be the morning*, Bea thought, as the dew was heavy on every blade of grass, making a cold as well as soft landing after a fall from Rusty, her magnificent allosaur. Bea tried to get up but she was held in place on the wet ground, unable to move. Rusty leant in to see if she was all right. So, yes, she must have fallen, that's why she was here on the ground. *There is no pain, that's good*, she thought. She wriggled her left hand free from under her and held it up to Rusty's face, patting him gently on his finely formed muzzle. 'I'm fine, I'm not hurt.' He licked her cheek as he usually did when he wanted another Mint Imperial. 'Sorry, Rusty, there are no more mints. You could do with one, you stink!' Bea giggled, as you do when a foul smell is funny just before it gets gross. She gently pushed Rusty away, 'Your breath seriously stinks, what have you been eating?'

Bea slowly opened her eyes from her long, deep sleep and blinked some reality into her dream.

A shadow raptor was peering into her hammock and she was stroking its face.

II

Knees Up Mother Brown

*~ let's all go down to the Strand,
'ave a banana ~*

Bea was fully awake in an instant. The large red raptor's face was looming over her and tilting from side to side, its sharp blue eyes blinking at her. Bea was relieved that these were not the strange haunting eyes she had seen before, but nonetheless they were very similar and petrifying to encounter. The raptor nudged her, making her swing in the hammock a little before peering in again and squawking, revealing its razor-sharp teeth.

'Don't move, Bea!' Theodore called out from behind her. He must have just woken as well. 'Bunty, wake up.' His words were soft but firm. 'Bunty, wake up but do not move!' he repeated.

There was a muffled reply and Theodore again tried to avoid the inevitable. 'Bunty, wake up but do not move or make a sound!'

But as Bea guessed, that was not going to happen.

Her grandmother pulled back the blanket that was

shielding her from the commotion, and peered out. Bunty shrieked and so did the shadow raptor, which quickly displayed its long ornate neck feathers. Bunty toppled out of her army camp bed onto the ground and rolled instantly back underneath it for safety.

'Theodore, get rid of it!'

'Easy now, Bunty. This is after all what we came to see, remember – Raptors of Paradise in the wild. Keep calm and no sudden movements, anyone. Let's see what it's up to.'

Theodore was holding out his hands towards the raptor in a gesture saying, *I'm unarmed; I have nothing for you.* He was keeping its attention and side-stepping it away from Bea and from where Bunty was quivering under her bed. 'Trust me, it's more scared of us, than we are of it.'

'That I find hard to believe,' muttered Bunty.

'Come here, boy, that's it, come here . . .' Theodore started to step backwards. Bea took in the full view: the shadow raptor was glorious. Its feather-covered body was mottled in shades of black and grey. Each individual feather caught the light and yet, instead of being glossy and reflective, in parts the plumes somehow swallowed its radiance and became matt, whereas in other parts it turned almost translucent. The dull black was not exactly black either: like Sammy's tail feather it was in fact deep green, making it almost disappear against the backdrop of the jungle. The raptor's legs were flanked along their length with short feathers; longer display plumes flared upwards from its ankles, much like bantam chickens back home. As the raptor turned Bea noticed that its long neck feathers were retracting, its face losing the angry red colour as it became calmer.

Theodore was making good progress leading the raptor towards him, over to the other side of the tree where Junior was tied, ignoring everyone. Bea remained motionless in her hammock as Theodore had commanded. As she peered out she realised the floor had been totally cleared: all the fallen leaves had been brushed between the deep buttress roots or pushed out beyond the perimeter of the tree's hanging branches. It was exactly as she had seen with the smaller Bluepan and she realised that this was probably the raptor's dance arena.

Bea calmly lifted her legs and swung them over the side of the hammock, standing in one movement. Theodore looked up. 'Bea, don't do anything silly.'

'It's his display arena,' she said softly, as the raptor looked sharply round at her, refilling its face with red. 'We're making it messy.'

Theodore looked about. 'Clever girl. What do you suggest we do?'

'Help it clear up?' Bea was sure of the situation but not of her solution. There was only one way to find out. She went over to one of Bunty's cases and tried to pick it up, then opted to simply push it away to the edge of the treeline.

'Grandma, can you get up and help?' Bea slid the camp bed away, revealing Bunty underneath, wide-eyed.

'Beatrice, this is no time to . . .'

'Bunty, get up and move your kit on the double,' Theodore commanded in his army voice.

Bunty sprang to attention and helped Bea tackle the last case.

'Okay, now what, my dear?' Bunty asked.

The raptor hopped over to where the kit had been and Bea and Bunty stepped towards Theodore standing by the trunk of the tree.

'Good work, Bea.'

'Look, it's getting its arena back to how it should be.' Bea smiled as the raptor brushed the ground with its foot feathers, removing all traces of the humans. 'And its face is pinkish grey,' she added, 'it's calmer.'

The raptor scampered about like this for another five minutes, inspecting and adjusting every stone until it was totally happy with its arena. Then it adopted a completely new posture, its head pulled right into its chest, its elbows out, sending an array of plumage out in an arc. The raptor stood still for a while, tilting its head side to side, checking everyone was watching before making its next move. It quickly hopped up and lifted both legs up so that they seemed to disappear into its plumage, then beat down hard with its wings, momentarily taking flight. The force of the flap raised a cloud of dust from the ground.

'So that's why it moves away the old leaves,' Bea whispered, and both Theodore and Bunty nodded in appreciation.

The raptor proceeded to leap on the spot a few times before pulling its next dance move. By stretching out its neck at the apex of the jump it got a few more inches' height. At the same time its face flashed from pink to red. This was truly the most privileged display that they had ever seen. Bunty's eyes welled up with happy tears.

With the last thump to the ground the raptor returned to its normal position and shook out a little wiggle.

'Do we clap now?' Bunty held her hand to her mouth.

Then something quite extraordinary happened. The shadow raptor partially opened its muzzle and from deep within it made a noise that somehow spoke: *Buuunty, waaake-up.*

They all froze.

Buunty, waake up, the raptor repeated and then, perfecting it a third time, *Bunty, wake up.*

All three of them stood in stunned silence, open-mouthed.

Theodore cleared his throat. 'Who's a pretty boy, then?'

The raptor looked straight at Theodore, tilted its head, held its jaw open and repeated it back. *Whoo's-a pretty-boy den?*

Bea burst out in laughter.

The raptor turned to Bea and laughed back at her again and again.

'Amazing.' Theodore spoke softly. 'A raptor that can mimic noises. I know many species of bird like parrots and lyrebirds can imitate noises, even crows back home, but I don't think this has ever been seen or heard of before.'

Suddenly Bea's mimicked laughter echoed from every direction. Flashes of red appeared from within the dark green foliage that surrounded the rainbow tree. One by one shadow raptors emerged and congregated under the rainbow tree's low canopy. The dancing raptor turned and bobbed its head up and down, greeting his fellow raptors with more of Bea's laughter until the sound swirled around them.

Bea moved a little closer to Theodore.

'Gosh, there seem to be quite a lot of them.' Bunty began to look quite concerned.

Bea squeezed into Theodore tightly and muttered, 'I don't like them all laughing, please make them stop.'

They were closing in as Theodore quickly assessed the situation.

'We are surrounded – at least a dozen, can't tell exactly how many as they all blend in.'

Bea swallowed hard. *Think, think,* she muttered to herself, *what would a raptor do?* Then a spark ignited in her head.

'Dance!'

'What?'

Bea looked at Bunty. 'Dance!'

'What, me?' Bunty said out of the side of her mouth and pointed to herself. 'I can't dance!'

'Er, not quite sure about that idea, Bea.' Theodore carefully unsheathed his machete.

The dancing raptor turned back and hopped uncomfortably close.

'Whoa, there's a good boy, get back now.' Theodore started talking soothing words but the creature dipped its head and nudged his midriff. 'Get back, I said.'

Ge-et baack.

With one hand on the hilt of his machete Theodore forcefully held out the other hand and pushed the raptor's muzzle away as it went in for another nudge.

In unison all the raptors lifted their fanned tails high and lowered their bright red faces, flaring their ice-blue eyes and hissing together.

Their reaction was alarming and Bea nervously looked down at the ground.

A muzzle nudged her back, and Bunty's too, pushing them away from the apparent safety of the tree trunk.

'Stay close . . .' Theodore pulled them towards him as the three of them tightened formation, back to back, all facing outwards.

The raptors continued to push and nudge.

'Theodore!'

'Hold tight, Bea!'

Bea looked up. They were surrounded by hissing shadow raptors.

Before Theodore could raise his machete again, Bunty whipped out her umbrella and quickly opened it out in front of her. 'Shoo, shoo, go on shoo!'

The raptors, stunned by this sudden movement, instantly froze and then fell over rigidly, their legs sticking straight out from their bodies. This caused a domino effect as they all toppled over one another. Theodore and Bea turned to Bunty, who grinned and continued to flap her brolly open and shut.

'Shoo, shoo!'

Theodore scratched his head. 'My word, Bunty!'

'Have you never seen a fainting goat before? Think it's called myotonic something-or-other. Not sure why they do it or how it works but it used to work on the farm animals so I thought it was worth a try.' She kept opening and shutting the umbrella. 'Apparently it's harmless.'

Theodore grabbed Bea's hand. 'Right, run for it!'

But as they started towards the opening a twitching raptor leg tripped Theodore up and they both fell on top of it.

Bunty turned. 'Get up, you two! I can't keep flapping this thing.'

But it was too late and the moment of opportunity had evaporated. Bunty continued to flap her brolly, but the raptors were now immune to the surprise. Again, they started closing in.

'Dance, come on!' yelled Bea. 'There's nothing else to try, dance for your life!'

Springing to her feet, Bea made the raptors all step back a few paces by flinging out her arms, opening up a small circle around her. She pirouetted on the spot and tried to recall her ballet classes move for move.

'Beatrice, I though you hated your ballet lessons!' Bunty exclaimed as she put away her umbrella. Theodore got to his feet and started clapping loudly. The raptors looked on intently.

'I can't keep this up all day!' Bea cried out on her fourth repetition.

'Theodore, help her!' Bunty called out. 'It's working, look – their faces are fading!'

'But I can't do ballet, Bunty!'

'Do anything! I don't know, sing something and jiggle about!'

To Bea's relief Theodore leapt into the circle and yelled out his Cockney cowboy battle cry, 'Alright, let's be 'avin ya!' and then through clenched teeth sang:

'There came a girl from France,
Who didn't know how to dance,
The only thing that she could do,
Was knees up Mother Brown.'

Bea looked on in amazement as Theodore proceeded to hook his thumbs under his braces, lift up his knees and dance.

'Oh, knees up Mother Brown,
Knees up Mother Brown,
Knees up, knees up, never let the breeze up,
Knees up Mother Brown!'

Bea and Bunty started to clap in time and smirked at each other as Theodore continued:

'Oh, hopping on one foot,
Hopping on one foot,

Hopping, hopping, never stopping,
Hopping on one foot!'

And as his tune suggested he hopped in time on one foot. Bea tried to hold back the laughter.

'Oh, knees up Mother Brown,
Knees up Mother Brown,
Knees up, knees up, never let the breeze up,
Knees up Mother Brown!'

'Oh, Theodore, I forgot you knew this song!' Bunty cheered him on.

'Oh, prancing up and down,
Prancing up and down,
Prancing, prancing, never dancing,
Prancing up and down!'

Theodore's dancing was too much of a ridiculous sight for Bea to contain herself any longer and she laughed out loud. Theodore had pranced close to Bunty and hooked his arm into hers, lifting her off her feet.

'Come on, Bunty!' he cried.

'Oh, whirling round and round,
Whirling round and round,
Whirling, whirling, never twirling,
Whirling round and round!'

The last time the two of them had danced like this the

war had just ended and now, despite everything, despite their current danger, it filled them both with happy memories as they sang the last verse together.

'Oooh myyy, what a rotten song,
What a rotten song,
What a rotten song,
Ooooh my, what a rotten song,
What a rotten singer toooo – oi!'

Side to side they clapped their hands together and spread them out with a triumphant and louder than normal 'Oi' at the end.

Theo swung Bunty back to him and Bea broke out clapping. 'More! What's that other song that goes "Let's all go down to the Strand, 'ave a banana"?'

'Come on now, Bea, that's enough,' said Theodore, breathing heavily.

'Bravo!' Bunty applauded.

Bravo-o-o! came the repetition from the raptors, who were all tilting their heads.

Bunty smiled shakily. 'Well, Theodore, if it all ends here today, at least we went out with a song and dance.'

Then, from above, came a mimicked echo of Theodore's voice.

'Kneeees up Mother Browwwwn?'

They looked up, and staring back at them were the cold blue eyes that had been following Bea for days. The eyes were surrounded by a bright red face embedded in a dark mass of feathers. The creature dropped from the low branch above them and landed, crouching to the ground in front of the three of them. The shadow raptors all took a step back and bowed their heads.

'*Knees up Mother Brown?*' it repeated again.

Shimmering its wings and twitching its leg feathers did not disguise the fact that this raptor was half as solid as the others and somewhat skinny and bedraggled. Bea had now become quite an expert on shadow raptors through her morning's experience and it was immediately obvious that this raptor's tail was very stunted and thinner than the others. Its foot and shin feathers flared out and spiked in the same way, but somehow without the finesse that she had admired on the raptor that had danced that morning. And then she noticed its claws . . . claws clasped in its . . . hands? The new raptor flipped back its black mass of long display feathers on top of its head and extended its neck.

'Is this another sort of Raptor of Paradise?' Bunty spoke out of the side of her mouth to Theodore beside her.

At that the creature pushed up from the floor and stood bolt upright. It stared directly at them.

Bea gasped. 'That's no raptor, it's a boy.'

12

I Can Close My Eyes

~ I can't close my ears ~

Christian Hayter leant back in his chair and kicked his boots up onto the end of his desk. He had things on his mind. Firstly maths. It was never his strongest subject as he often ran out of fingers to count on but things were not adding up. The latest batch of colourful Raptors of Paradise were definitely smaller and lighter than usual. A short Javanese man came in through the swing doors with the last cage in his arms and landed it on the oversized cast-iron scales, sending a dust cloud up in the air.

'One hundred and eighty pounds.' He looked back at Hayter.

'You sure?'

'Scales don't lie: one hundred and eighty pounds.'

'Make it two hundred.'

'How?'

'Wet them, feed them stones – I don't care, make it two hundred.' Hayter slammed his fist onto the desk, jolting everything on it into the air. It was getting harder

and harder to find enough raptors to meet demand; he was having to send hunters deeper into the jungle to get them, and this cost more.

Then there was his other problem, but this was about to be solved: the swing doors swooshed open and in fell an out-of-breath Bishop.

'Boss, boss!' He fell to his knees, exhausted.

'I sent you two fools out days ago, what are you doing back here already?'

'Boss, boss . . .'

'YES – what?'

Bishop rested his hands on his knees and panted. 'Boss, I've ridden that donkey all night.'

'SO . . . WHAT, you idiot?'

'Out on the old spice trail, we found the remains of a fire.'

Hayter looked at Bishop and rolled his eyes. 'And?'

'Ash picked up some interesting prints, one was definitely from a woman.'

Hayter became instantly alert. 'How sure is he?'

'Well, unless it's a small man wearing pointed shoes. And the place smelt a bit like, what did he say – ammonia . . . is that a kind of perfume, boss?'

Hayter stood up quickly, swung the chair round and grabbed his jacket off the back of it.

'Run down to the bar, round up the men – we're all leaving right now!'

The Javanese man looked up. 'All of us?'

'No, Jong, you fatten up the other raptors and start shifting this noisy lot down to the dock,' Hayter ordered, gesturing to the cages that now almost filled the large depot. 'This shipment heads out on the cargo boat on time, you got it?'

✦ ✦ ✦

Leaving right now actually took over an hour. You can't go charging into the jungle without important kit like water and rifles, and a few stashed bottles of *arak*, the local booze that fuelled everything, including lanterns.

'Move it, you louts!' Hayter barked impatiently at the men as they saddled up four mimus, three fresh donkeys and two young and sprightly prickleback kylos that could keep up with the pace.

Riding fast along the wide and well-maintained trade paths gave Hayter an advantage. But as soon as daylight faded they had to pace it carefully, looking out for the places where the old paths criss-crossed and where Bishop had left markers for his return. Eventually the dark trails, dimly lit by the orange glow of their lanterns, gave way to the clearing in which Bea had sprung the raptor trap.

Where bright daylight had been able to penetrate the jungle floor, that evening's moonlight was able to enlighten Hayter's surroundings. The blue tinted moonshine made everything sparkle like a frost-covered morning and he was able to see clearly around him without the need of his lantern. In the centre of the enchanted-looking space was Ash, asleep in front of a glowing fire. As Hayter drew closer Ash jolted awake and raised his rifle.

'Ash, fill me in. What or who have you found?'

'They're still close, boss, and they're not covering their tracks, so it's easy to follow.'

'How many of them?'

'Bit confused as they're riding a kylos, so not all tracks are present all of the time, but definitely one woman, one heavy-set man and one child.'

'A child?' Hayter pondered. 'They said nothing about a child being with them back at the depot. Anyhow, good work. Do you reckon if we set off before dawn, we could catch them sleeping?'

'Easy,' Ash confirmed.

'What on earth has happened here, anyway? Did we catch something?' Hayter looked around him, taking in the triggered raptor trap.

'No, boss. This is after I cleared it up. It was a right state. I've re-laid the snares but the big one was triggered and then cut into bits – it's totally unusable now.'

'Logan,' Hayter said. 'I knew he was here to cause trouble and not to shop – should have got rid of him alongside his pet phalox years ago and saved me the trouble now.'

'What about the lady, boss?'

'I can't let her find the answers to the questions she's asking about the Kingsleys – it would be very bad for business, mine and the big man's. He won't be happy that there are loose ends after all these years. I have to find out what she knows.'

'And the kid?'

'What about the kid? There are plenty of orphans out there.'

+ + +

Dawn was just as idyllic in the clearing as the moonlight had been, but the men did not notice as they prepared to leave: enthusiastic drinking of the homemade spirit *arak* dulled every morning. It was not long after they had started tracking that Hayter signalled with his hand for silence. Everybody stopped.

The jungle is never silent, but over their heavy breathing and the myriad animal noises, Hayter picked up something faint and very unusual. He turned his head fractionally and closed his eyes to focus, dampening the background noises to single it out.

'Laughter! It's laughter coming from that way.'
Further up the path Hayter suddenly stopped, the rest
of his gang concertinaing behind him, banging into each
other on the slippery path. He turned around and gave
a menacing look back at them all, holding his finger to
his lips.

Again he held his breath and closed his eyes to find
the direction of laughter, but everything was now silent.
He tilted his head left and then right, but nothing.

'You can't have gone, I know you're still there,' he
muttered to himself as the men shrugged at each other.
Hayter breathed in, tasting the air and narrowed his eyes.
'Hang on. The laughter may have gone, but what's that?'
He closed his eyes once more and refocused, picking away
the bird and insect chatter till he located the new sound.

Opening his eyes wide and locking on his new direction he stared ahead.

'Men, ready your rifles. We have shadow raptors, lots of them, and they're hissing. You know what that means. They are about to attack.'

They all quickly loaded up, taking a slug of *arak* each for courage. Ash passed it to Hayter last of all, but he brushed it aside.

'I'll celebrate after we make the kill. I want Parker, Brett and Dallas flanking on my left, Hudson and Hicks, you two go with Ash and stay on my right. Bishop, you, Drake and Vasquez hang back here with the rest of you lot and fan out, find suitable cover, dig in and wait. We're going round them wide so we can flush them back up to you lot here, got it?'

The men nodded.

'And wait for my signal.'

'What's the signal, boss?' Bishop asked.

'A clan of shadow raptors running your way, screeching. When they're close pick them off one by one – don't use a blanket of bullets; we'll be right behind them.'

Hayter looked at his men and noticed the almost empty bottle in Ash's hand.

'Actually, chaps –' he thought for a moment – 'we need to catch what we can, don't kill them. Some of you have not been hitting your quotas. The cargo ship has space on board, let's fill it up with live shadow raptors.'

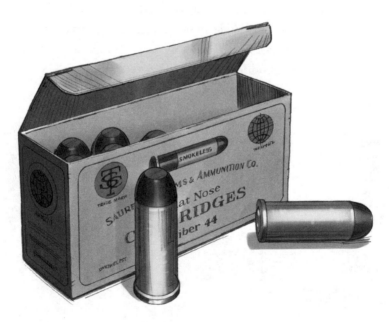

Bishop and his men laced together some ropes and impromptu nets whilst the others set off.

'What about the woman? And I saw kids' prints as well, boss?' Ash quietly reminded Hayter.

'I'm taking down the man and rounding the others up,' Hayter told him. 'You lot are only after the raptors, understand me? That man Logan is mine.'

It did not take long for everyone to fall into place. Hayter's instincts were spot on and led him right to a part of the jungle where the low line of fauna was trampled and broken, but as usual the raptors' tracks had been swept by the feathers on their feet so there was no knowing how many of them there were. The shadow raptors' camouflaged feathers were perfectly evolved to blur into the background, cloaking them from the eyes of their prey. But to someone like Hayter, who knew what to look for, they could be spotted. 'Look for blank patches without flowers and branches,' he had briefed his men. But this time something was strange. The men could all clearly hear the raptors' hissing up close, and on top of that, the sound of someone clapping their hands to a beat.

Hayter signalled to the men on his left and right, two fingers pointing to his eyes then out to where he thought was the centre of the action. They gave him a shrug to say they could not see anything. Then, to add to the frustration, the singing started. All the other men looked back at Hayter, who was now seething. This was not only a song he knew very well, but the Cockney voice singing it was the man he was hunting: Theodore Logan.

'I'll give you "Knees Up Mother Brown" you dirty toe rag! Where are you hiding,' he muttered to himself. His open hand signal told the men to sit tight as he moved out from cover. Crouching down, he scuttled over to a new vantage point close to a large overhanging rainbow eucalyptus and scanned the ground around him but there was nothing. Hayter knew that from here he should see some signs of life, of the blank patches where raptors waited, but there was just an expanse of jungle around the large tree.

Returning to the men he sat puzzled as a woman's voice joined in the last chorus.

> 'Oooh myyy, what a rotten song,
> What a rotten song,
> What a rotten song,
> Ooooh my, what a rotten song
> What a rotten singer toooo – oi!'

Hayter sat still, back turned away from the rainbow tree, and closed his eyes. *Do I trust my ears, or my eyes?* He rocked forward and concentrated. *I can close my eyes, but I can't close my ears.* He spun round and held his hand up, clenched it into a fist then pointed it at the tree. The attack was about to start. He raised his rifle to his cheek and aimed straight at the tree in front of him. As before, Hayter cut away the background noise and focused his mind and aim on the voices. And there it was: not as deep as before but it sure sounded like Logan.

'Knees up, Mother Brown?'

Hayter breathed in deeply, aimed his rifle towards the voice and squeezed the trigger.

13

Fly For Your Life

~ *extreme slow motion* ~

The gunshot split the air, startling everything under the rainbow tree. *Guns? Who's shooting?* thought Bea, panicking, and she watched the boy's eyes widen as he started to fall forwards towards her. In Bea's terrified mind what happened next passed in extreme slow motion.

A second shot rang out, seeming to move so slowly that Bea could see the red-hot bullet cut through the morning air, evaporating the moisture in its path and leaving a vapour trail behind as it sliced past the boy – only just missing Bea. The bullet finally impacted the tree behind her, resonating deeply, but her attention was on the boy looming towards her. The raptors had heard the shot and by the time the second was making its way past Bea they were already beating a retreat. The boy reached out and grabbed her arms, forcing her backwards, their faces only about an inch apart. A third bullet whistled overhead, slicing through where she had been standing only a fraction of a second ago. Just like yesterday, this strange creature, this boy, was again saving her life like a guardian angel.

With plenty of time to brace herself Bea finally landed on the ground but she had to wait even longer for the boy to land on top of her, shielding her from harm. He had positioned them between the same two deep buttress roots that only yesterday Bea had sat on, looking at her father's name in his book that named the tree and reading her mother's last letter. Yesterday felt like years ago.

More gunshots spiralled through the air and hit the tree above, sending a shower of mossy splinters of bark floating gracefully onto them. The boy looked deeply into Bea's eyes as if he was looking into her soul. Slowly they blinked together – and in that instant the world around Bea sped up again.

The raptors flew in every direction as more bullets rang out. The boy rolled off Bea. In front of them Bunty spun as Theodore flew back a pace and then staggered, clutching his shoulder. Staring into his blood-soaked hand he slumped and fell. Bunty dived to Theodore's side, trying to get an arm under his body to lift him, but he was too heavy. She ripped the lace cuff from her sleeve and forced it into the open wound that was spurting blood. It was not enough to stop the rapid flow.

The boy sprang up from the shelter of the tree's buttresses just as Hayter and two of his men charged.

'What kind of raptor is that? Don't shoot it, I want it alive!' Hayter screamed as he leapt over and shoulder-barged the feathered boy into a spin at full force. Both man and boy landed with a thud, close to the stricken Theodore. As Hayter scrabbled to his feet Bunty laid into him with all her frustration, anger, and with her umbrella.

'Don't shoot that child! Leave him alone, you thug!' screamed Bunty. 'Stop killing everything!'

Hayter had one very simple reply, formed by his left arm swinging down and striking her cleanly. He watched Bunty fly backwards and land next to her motionless friend. A satisfied grin appeared on his face, but as he turned the grin vanished. The raptor creature was disappearing into the jungle.

The bullets were now flying well beyond the tree and were laced with the screeching of wounded shadow raptors. Bea stood up from her high-sided tree-root bunker and witnessed the carnage all around. The shadow raptors lay where they had fallen; she saw Theodore spread out on the floor and Bunty sobbing over him. She saw Hayter racing back towards her, leaping the high tree roots before him. Just like the shadow raptor boy before her, she dived into the jungle undergrowth.

Hayter raced after her, deep into the forest, but Bea was one step ahead, lit up with adrenaline, bolting as far away as she could. Dipping, weaving, jumping and skidding over, under, anything to get away from the hell that was happening behind her.

◆ ◆ ◆

It was quite a while later that Hayter reappeared under the rainbow tree, panting heavily and followed by Hudson and Hicks, dragging a dead shadow raptor behind them. Bunty, still at Theodore's side, looked up; a shudder of relief passed over her shocked white face upon seeing that Bea was not with him.

'Ash, take her away. She's getting on my nerves.' Hayter gestured towards Bunty.

'Bishop's bagged about a dozen, boss – a good day's hunting,' Ash said, as he pulled Bunty to her feet.

Hayter said nothing but slung his rifle over his shoulder.

'That hunch paid off, boss. From where I was hiding this tree was empty – how did you see anything?'

Hayter spat on the ground. 'I saw nothing, like you.'

'Seriously? Nah, pull the other one. You were bang on target!'

Hayter then did what Ash had tried to do with Bishop the day before and impress him with an air of mystery. However, unlike Bishop, Hayter was telling the truth.

'I shot at a ghost.'

Hayter moved around the tree, running his hand over the trunk, finding a freshly gouged bullet strike that had splintered the colourful bark. He pulled off a section.

'There's something familiar about this place, this tree . . . you ever been here before, Ash?'

Ash looked up from loading Theodore's kit onto Junior and shrugged.

Examining the bark, Hayter found a deep scar, older than the bullet strike, that had grown around something stuck in the tree. Hayter pulled out his bullhook, jabbed its sharp point into the trunk and dug it out in a few easy scrapes. Holding it up between his fingers, it became obvious what had caused the tree to scar. He was holding a bullet.

Today was not the only shootout that had taken place under this tree. Hayter flicked the bullet up into the air and caught it again.

'That woman knows something. Why else would she be here, under this of all trees?' he muttered to himself. Then, out loud: 'Ash, camp back at the clearing with all this kit. Leave that one to rot here.' He pointed at Theodore. 'And I want answers from that woman, got it?'

Hayter stepped back a good few paces, looking directly at the spot where he had removed the old bullet from the tree trunk. He raised an imaginary rifle with both hands and squinted down the sights at the bullet hole. 'Hang on,' he muttered. 'It was a revolver.'

He dropped the imaginary rifle and raised just his right hand, now holding a new imaginary pistol, and took aim. 'Bang, bang, you're dead.' The pistol recoiled as Hayter acted out the scenario in his head. He watched his victims fall to the ground as he walked over, spinning the phantom pistol around his finger with a grin on his face. Looking down at the dirt, he kicked the bare ground that had been swept by a shadow raptor now slumped dead a few paces away. 'Gone, Franklin. The saurs you tried to protect devoured every last scrap of you, they didn't even leave the bones.'

Hayter looked around him but the dirt had nothing to reveal except smears of fresh blood.

'Lost something, boss?'

'No, Ash. Just shooting more ghosts.'

14

A Long Way From Home

~ Kunava ~

Bea fell to her knees in the mud with a squelch. She was exhausted and dripping with sweat, a mess of hair clinging to her face. It was hard to catch her breath in the hot humid air and something was blocking her airway. Feeling faint, she retched and spat out a multitude of bugs that she had inhaled in her desperate dash away from the gunshots and screams.

Her lungs were ablaze, screaming out for oxygen, and at last she was able to fill them with a deep breath. But, like dosing fire with fuel, this sparked another bout of retching and coughing until her throat was red-raw. Slumped forward, she tried to focus on her breathing, her eyes filling with tears.

It took a while before she was breathing more steadily and feeling calmer. Sitting back, Bea took stock of the situation. Her clothes were shredded with patches of blood soaking through where low branches and coarse vines had whipped and ripped at her. She pulled herself out of the mud and sat up on a tree root, pulling off a leech that was just about to get stuck into her arm.

'Focus,' she muttered to herself. 'Think, think . . .'

So much had happened. Bea tried to rebuild the morning's events one by one. It was not long ago she had been safely in a dreamworld, before she was woken by a very close encounter with a shadow raptor that proceeded to dance for them. Then it had mimicked her laughter, the other raptors joining in and crowding around the three of them until they all had to have a turn dancing. Perhaps the raptors' behaviour was not as intimidating and threatening as she had thought at the time. Bea had had similar experiences back in England when she was walking across a field and all the cows had gathered and surrounded her. Perhaps it was just curiosity.

Then the strange raptor boy had risen up before her, and the ambush by hunters and then . . . her eyes widened and a shiver went down her spine as the next vision swam into her mind. Theodore! He was down, covered in blood – could he be dead? And Grandma, she had been hit by that man. Was she all right? Was she dead too?

'Think . . . think.'

The screams she had heard – that was Bunty screaming, cursing someone called Hayter. Could Bunty still be alive? But where? The hunters could be taking her back to the port. Bea needed to get back there – better still, to Sammy and Biggie's house in the Old Town to get help. She looked around her at the dense foliage. Which way should she go? Bea could not even be sure of the direction that she had just run from. How on earth would she ever get out?

'Focus, focus.'

Taking her hands from her face she anxiously patted her neck, wanting to hold her locket, to see if her parents could comfort her. Then real panic set in. The locket was gone. She was truly alone.

With her heart pounding Bea dropped again to her knees, desperately scanning and patting the forest floor around her, tossing away fallen leaves. The focus that had been holding her together was gone; the short, panicked breathing returned, along with the flood of tears.

Crack. A branch snapped a short distance away, sending a chilling shudder over her entire body that instantly froze every droplet of sweat. Had she not run far enough? Was this how her parents had disappeared? Lost for days deep in the jungle, with no idea which way was out . . . and then hunted? Hunched low to the ground, Bea looked around to find somewhere to run to, but her body was locked with fear; she knew it was pointless. Running was not going to solve this.

Crack. This time it was closer.

Crouching low, Bea had a good line of sight under the foliage in front of her and her eyes darted back and forth. She was panicking, but what she saw relieved her greatly. It was another Raptor of Paradise – but without

Sammy next to her its name remained a mystery. This one was smarter and longer than the comical Bluepan with its strange fleshy horns, and this raptor's bright yellow legs made it easy to spot under the green ferns. It dipped its head low, revealing jet black eyes set against a bright yellow face and a thick collar of golden neck feathers dashed with black. It slowly moved forward, revealing its scarlet chest and long, dark blue forelimb feathers. Trailing behind it was a flamboyant and almost impossibly long tail of more golden, red and dark blue feathers. Its tail was almost twice as long as its neck and body and it pulsated and opened like a fan.

Suddenly the raptor stopped as they both heard another *crack*, this time very close. The raptor looked past Bea at something standing behind her. In an instant it puffed its forelimb

feathers out wide and lifted its tail then fanned it out fully, like a peacock, instantly magnifying its appearance in a dazzling display.

Toot, toot! it called out.

Something whistled past and hit the raptor bang in the middle of its chest, knocking it backwards with a force that sent golden feathers up into the air, its legs twitching as if it was running away. Before Bea could feel any more scared, the raptor's killer spoke.

'You lost,' a strange voice called out. 'You a long way from home.' Bea pulled herself up and, still looking at the ground, turned to face whoever was behind her.

She saw two bare feet and legs, splattered with mud, and as Bea followed them upwards she realised that the man facing her was an indigenous tribesman. His skin was covered with a mixture of yellow and red ochre body paint in great swirls; circling his waist was a thin cord that supported a hollowed-out gourd hanging between his legs.

In one hand he held a small shield made from kylosaur plates edged with cowrie shells and ferns, and in the other was a bow and three long, slender arrows. As the man squatted down to face Bea she realised that what he lacked in clothing he made up for with his enormous headdress. It was almost like a top hat, but made entirely from feathers from the same sort of golden raptor that had just stood in front of her.

'You looking for your parents?'

He tilted his head; it shimmered with an orange glow. Bea could barely make sense of this strange question.

'Yes,' she breathed eventually.

'Good. I think I've found them.' The tribesman smiled, revealing his betel-nut-stained teeth, and spat out bright red saliva that landed on a large green leaf.

'You have found my parents?' Bea could hardly believe her ears.

The man kept grinning in a way that filled Bea with confidence that he did not mean any harm to her.

'I'm Kunava.' He held out his hand but when Bea looked down she saw that his feathered wristband had two large raptor claws bound to it where his hand should have been. Bea had seen pictures of pirates with hooks for hands but this was something much more deadly. Dangling from one claw was her silver necklace and locket.

'Oh! My locket!' Bea reached out and unhooked it from

his claw. Remembering some manners she looked away from the thing she so obviously wanted to keep staring at. 'I'm Bea,' she smiled. 'I cannot thank you enough.'

The man said nothing, but nodded and then moved past her. He leant over the raptor that had fallen on its back and turned it over. Holding it down with his claw-hand he worked down its tail to its behind and located the base of one of its long feathers. He turned to Bea, still grinning.

'You can help, come here.'

Bea crouched down next to him.

'Hold it down onto the ground, with both hands. This can get tricky with my claw.'

Bea replaced his claws with both her hands.

'Why do we need to hold onto it?'

'It's going to wake up and not be happy.'

'Wake up? But it's dead!'

'Oh no, not dead – stunned. My arrow had no point, I didn't want to kill it.'

Bea was puzzled, but held on a bit tighter as Kunava yanked out one of the raptor's extra-long tail feathers. It woke immediately with a loud *Tooooooot!*

'Hold it steady . . .'

As the raptor tried to flap about, he quickly located the end of another feather and gave another yank.

Tooooooot! it cried out again.

'Okay, you can let it go.'

Bea did as she was told. The raptor righted itself and with a flurry of feathers made its way quickly out of arms' reach.

Kunava looked at his two new long feathers and grinned even more widely. Bea picked up a few of the smaller feathers that had dropped in the commotion and saw Kunava's arrow.

'Here.' She offered it back to him.

He held it up to her. 'See, it has a cork end. Won't hurt a bit. You can keep the feathers.'

'Thank you.' Bea took them from him, wiping her mouth.

'Thirsty?'

'Very!' Bea replied and Kunava beamed his betel-red smile back at her. Things were looking up.

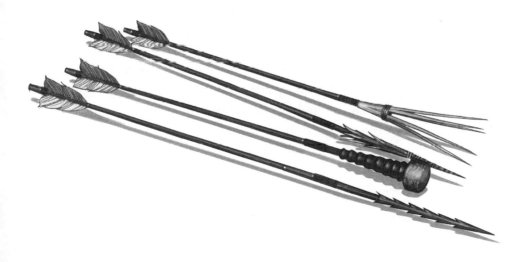

15

Savaged Alive

~ *a tasty snack at night* ~

Theodore groaned and slowly fluttered his eyelids awake. He was wrapped up somehow and being pulled along the forest floor, he thought, but it was too dark to know for sure. He tried to reach out but his body reacted sharply in immense pain; and anyway he was too tightly bound. He sank back to his unconscious state.

+ + +

Over the years the raptor boy had made his nest out of stolen items better suited to his needs than those of his fellow raptors. A groundsheet and an old, large canvas kit bag that had once belonged to one of the hunters formed a bed of sorts. The kit bag hung from a low branch in the tree, with the groundsheet wrapped around and over it to form a barrier against wind and rain. At night the boy would climb into the kit bag and use it like a cocoon, just like the moths and butterflies he had observed. Cleverly this arrangement also reduced exposure to the thousands of bugs that came out at night; it protected him from everything . . . except snakes. He still had not worked out a way to stop them being curious and slipping down the rope that suspended the kit bag, but in turn he had found that they did offer a tasty snack at night.

The boy knew that the human urgently needed his help, which he could only give properly back at his secluded nest. Knowing that humans prefer to lie down, having spied on many before, he bent over two young saplings and forced their leafy tops into a large grain sack that had once been Biggie's a long time ago. Stuffing the sack full and bending the saplings down to the ground, he snapped them at the base and made quite a good makeshift nest to rest the human on.

The other raptors looked on, twitching and tilting their heads, commenting with a *kwaaark* every now and then as the boy worked. He carefully rolled the human over and onto the sack and got him as comfortable as he could. The boy paused as the human groaned again but did not wake up. He gathered some short sections of rope and bound the

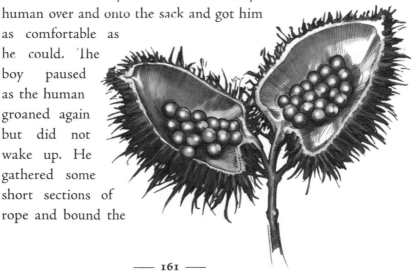

human's wrists tightly to the sapling trunks now forming the sides of his bed. He did the same around his waist and ankles.

Buttons baffled him so he took out one of the raptor claws that were always kept wedged in his waistband and ripped open the human's blood-soaked shirt. There was a deep wound above his chest that the boy immediately spat onto and ran his fingers over, smearing the blood around. He then sucked on two of his fingers and rubbed them with his thumb before checking back to find the exit hole.

Theodore jolted forward with pain as the boy stuck his fingertip into the wound.

The boy turned to the raptors behind him and squawked. They all squawked back in time together and closed in tightly. Popping his raptor claw in his mouth to suck on it first, the boy carefully dug the tip of the claw into the bullet hole and opened it up with the precision of a surgeon.

Theodore's eyes electrified awake as the claw dug deeper. Waking to the excruciating pain was not the worst thing, however. Theodore's eyes widened at the realisation that he was being clawed in front of a dozen salivating shadow raptors. Before he could scream, the raptor boy shoved a stubby stick in his mouth. He lifted up the scabbed blood and skin around the wound. Seething in pain, Theodore bit down hard as the boy looked over his handiwork before spitting directly into the freshly opened

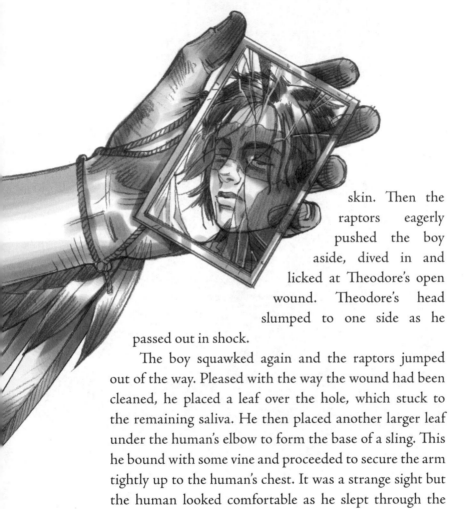

skin. Then the raptors eagerly pushed the boy aside, dived in and licked at Theodore's open wound. Theodore's head slumped to one side as he passed out in shock.

The boy squawked again and the raptors jumped out of the way. Pleased with the way the wound had been cleaned, he placed a leaf over the hole, which stuck to the remaining saliva. He then placed another larger leaf under the human's elbow to form the base of a sling. This he bound with some vine and proceeded to secure the arm tightly up to the human's chest. It was a strange sight but the human looked comfortable as he slept through the pain. The human would need his wound dressing again soon but he would survive.

The boy's thoughts turned to the other humans.

When he had returned to the rainbow tree, he had found only Theodore. The strange girl cub and the alpha woman were gone. It was not hard to follow the tracks and he instinctively knew where the attackers were heading. Many of the raptor boy's clan lay dead around the tree, but many more were missing – they must also be with the hunters. There was only one thing to do. The hunters had brought the war to the raptors' display arena: now it was time to take it to theirs. The boy pulled out a small broken mirror from some of his stolen possessions and looked at his cracked reflection. His red face was fading so he darted out to retrieve some achiote fruit. He crushed it up in a shell and smeared the bright red paste on with the help of his crude mirror.

Now looking the part, he summoned the remaining clan together with shrieks that pulsated until they had all joined in, bobbing their heads up and down and beating their forearm feathers in a frenzy. The boy stood in the centre and held out his arms, touching all the raptors on their muzzles and chanting rhythmically with them till he stood tall and shrieked out:

'Ayyy ayyyy ayyyy ayyyyy!'

With that they all darted off from the nest, leaving Theodore alone to sleep off his ordeal.

16

The Almighty
Stare of Stares

~ processed saurmeat ~

When Theodore awoke it was with an almighty headache and a parched mouth. He looked around him but saw no sign of any raptors. Perhaps he had dreamed it. He rolled over onto his good side and as he did so became aware of the green sling that bound his injured arm. He saw that next to the bed, or whatever the contraption was, stood a stump of wood like a bedside table with a small jerry can on it. He grabbed it and flipped off the top, quenching his burning thirst. Wiping the overspill off his moustache with his cuff he placed the jerry can back and as he did so he noticed a small flower that had been plucked and wedged into the bark. He looked more carefully around him.

On the mud floor below were hundreds of light grey, downy feathers. To one side of him was a tree with a variety of things strung up in cargo netting, including groundsheets and kit bags. Littered below it were all sorts of unrelated objects, ranging from empty wooden cases, coils of rope, some rags of clothing, a saddle and lots of army ration tins of SPAW. On the trunk of the tree were many small, dark red handprints and some ochre marks that looked almost like stick men and trees.

Theodore rose to his feet and tried to walk. His blade was over by the trunk and his hat was on a low branch next to the pile of SPAW tins. He picked up one that was not opened and inspected the label. A churning hunger filled his belly: he tried to fiddle one-handed with the winding key to open it but quickly opted to stabbing it with his knife. The processed saurmeat had a familiar salty smell that normally turned his stomach, but on this day was very welcome.

'Hello, is anybody home?' he called out. Behind the tree there were about a dozen rounded mounds made from many layers of sticks and ferns. Finishing off the tin and discarding it with the others he stepped over to investigate. Between and around the raised

nest mounds were a series of similar-sized shallow ditches with no ferns or sticks but more than the usual flecks of downy feathers inlaid into the dirt.

'Male shadow raptors must sleep around the edge of the nest and protect the female in the centre. Clever,' he muttered to himself.

Theodore looked into one raised nest with a perfectly presented clutch of eggs on some fresh ferns. Without thinking he dipped in and picked one up. It was still warm: big mistake.

A *hisssssssss!* came from behind and Theodore froze. Carefully placing the egg down exactly as he had found it, he turned to see a shadow raptor giving him the almighty stare of stares.

'Easy now, nothing's broken, my mistake.' He stepped back a few paces and fell backwards into one of the pits.

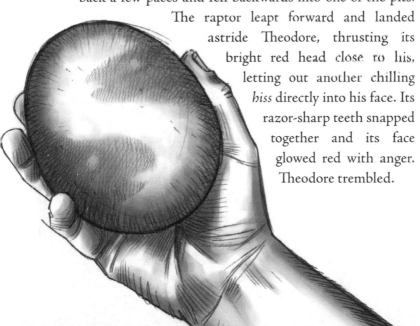

The raptor leapt forward and landed astride Theodore, thrusting its bright red head close to his, letting out another chilling *hiss* directly into his face. Its razor-sharp teeth snapped together and its face glowed red with anger. Theodore trembled.

He had somehow survived being savaged alive by a pack of deadly shadow raptors but now he had upset a brooding female. Suddenly, as it sniffed, it was alerted to Theodore's makeshift sling. The raptor nudged it once and then stood back. Theodore gulped and saw this opportunity to calmly try to get up.

The raptor swiftly moved in front of its clutch of eggs, issuing another long *hiss* at Theodore, who decided this was the best moment to leg it out of there. He turned to see if he was being followed, only to hit his head on a low-hanging wasps' nest, releasing a cloud of angry wasps. Flailing his one good arm around to ward them off, Theodore now had an even greater reason to run faster, dipping and swerving to avoid anything else that might hamper his escape from the swarm.

A giant bird-eating spider had been hoping for a good catch that day and had spun itself a mighty fine web that spanned the gap between two trees – and which Theodore blindly ran straight into. He managed to punch his way out but the spider's silky sticky thread had wrapped itself well around his face, and, unable to see, he ran a few more paces and straight into a tree with a thud.

Dazed, Theodore sat up and pulled the rest of the web off his face, only to get another shock. A short indigenous tribesman sporting a head full of brightly coloured feathers stood in front of him with a bright red smile. The man leant forward over Theodore's wounded shoulder and gave it a deep sniff, then winked back at him. He then laid down his bow and shield, held up two fingers and tapped the wound.

Theodore yelped like a puppy, then suddenly stopped in astonishment. 'Blimey! Its the only thing that doesn't hurt.'

The man didn't say anything. Just squatted on his haunches, and continued to grin at Theodore.

'Me, Theodore. The-o-dore. You?' Theodore pointed to himself with his one good hand, then held it out for a response from the man.

A high voice chirped from behind him.

'This is my friend Kunava and you don't need to talk to him like a child, he can understand you just fine.'

Wearing a bright set of colourful feathers in a tribal headband, Bea looked quite spectacular and it made up for the tattered state of her clothing.

'Bea, you're safe!' Theodore scrambled to his feet and enveloped her in a bearhug. As she pulled away, Bea found that a lot of the sticky spiderweb had now annoyingly transferred over to her.

'Where's Bunty?'

'I don't know. That hunter probably has her.' Bea's face showed her anxiety. 'And I thought YOU were dead!' With that Bea burst into tears.

Kunava took hold of Theodore's arm and pulled off a large and angry-looking spider with his other claw-hand.

With that, he beckoned over his shoulder to the rest of his fearsome-looking tribesmen. Each had a different feathered headdress and was armed with bow, arrow and spears; each shared the same body paint and a steely expression. One passed Theodore an old hip flask.

Putting his arm around Kunava's shoulder, Theodore took a long swig.

'Nice to meet you, Kunava. Hello, chaps.' He lifted the flask and drenched his mouth again.

'My boys won't understand you. I used to live in the Old Town, picked up English from some traders. Then the Dutchman vanished and that depot started its horrible trade, so I moved back here to do what I can to look after the jungle, but it's a tough job.'

Kunava spat a mouthful of red betel nut to the floor so he could continue.

'We heard the gunfire but we had to stand back – our arrows and darts are no match for angry bullets.'

'Are you okay?' Bea prodded Theodore's green sling.

'I am – which is so strange. The raptor boy we met, I thought he was torturing me with his claw . . . well, he was, kind of . . . definitely felt like torture for sure, and then the shadow raptors were trying to eat me, but they didn't. And now here I am, healing nicely. It's all very strange.'

'Same thing happened to me a good few years back and the shadows sorted me out,' Kunava told him. 'Mine will take longer to heal.' He lifted his claw-hand.

Bea stared at it again while Theodore wiped his brow and continued his tale.

'I woke today with this homemade sling on and all the raptors had left the nest except for one very upset female who . . . er, didn't like the way I was . . . holding one of her eggs.'

Kunava whistled. 'Whooooooo, don't you know anything? Never mess with a female raptor and her eggs!'

Theodore felt foolish. 'I know, I know, but I wasn't thinking straight.'

'This tough young lady has been helping us get ready – you think you're up for it?'

'Up for what?' Theodore patted himself down.

'Reckon we've got some hunting to do.'

17

Trouble in Paradise

~ the vale of shadows ~

'If you think I'm going to say a word to you then you're sorely mistaken, you horrid little pig!' Despite the defiance in her voice, Bunty's tear-stained face, angry red eyes and ripped clothing painted a pathetic picture. With her hands tied together and tethered to a tree it was pointless to try to escape, and besides, where would she go?

'Tea?' Hayter offered her one of the steaming hot tin mugs he was holding. 'Go on, it won't kill you.' He held it out. Every inch of Bunty's body wanted to refuse it but she was so dehydrated and hungry she could not bring herself to turn it down.

'It might not kill me, but you probably will.'

Hayter stood uncomfortably close and shoved one of the mugs into her hands.

'Depends if you have the right answers to my questions.'

'I was the one who broke all those nasty snares you set.' Bunty tried to get the upper hand and motioned towards the broken trap at the centre of the clearing, now busy with Hayter's men lashing the muzzles of the recently captured shadow raptors. 'And I would do it again if I were to have the chance.'

Hayter stood back and took a sip of his tea.

'So you're the one causing all the trouble in paradise. Thanks for that, and thanks also for leading me straight to a clan of shadow raptors. Only wish I'd had more men and nets with me so I could have caught the lot of them.'

Bunty looked to the ground and said nothing.

Hayter got straight into his line of questioning. 'The people you want to find, what makes you think they came to the Islands of Aru?'

'They came to see the amazing wildlife that you're taking from this island. I'm surprised there is any left after all these years,' Bunty retorted.

'And you think that breaking my traps is going to stop all that, eh? So who are these people to you – why are they so important to find?'

Bunty took her first sip of tea to give her time to compose her answer.

'You don't look like a man who has a family, Mr Hayter.'

'No, no, I don't, very much over-rated in my opinion.'

'Then you wouldn't understand.'

'So the girl that ran away, is that Logan's daughter?'

'No, the man we are looking for is her father.'

'You know, she won't survive the night alone, that I can promise.'

Bunty's shoulders sank and she looked mournfully into her tea.

'Your kind of people don't last long out here – you think it's a barrel of laughs, let's all go and visit the pretty raptors!' Hayter mocked.

'Trust me, Mr Hayter, this is no laughing matter!'

'I heard you all laughing your heads off under that tree. Giving it all a sing-song, a right old knees-up you were having!' Hayter swilled out his empty mug. 'And what was that other feathered creature?'

Bunty looked up at him. 'How should I know?'

'Liar. What was it? A juvenile raptor?'

Bunty shrugged her shoulders. 'It jumped out of the tree and then you started shooting.'

'LIAR!' Hayter turned up the tone from uncomfortable to unbearable. 'You've got one last chance, lady. What was that feathered creature? It looked more like a boy than a raptor to me, and you said "Don't shoot the child".'

'Beatrice, my granddaughter – she's the child!' Bunty was struggling to backtrack.

'The other child, the one with the red face and feathers!' Hayter shouted.

'Listen to yourself! And you are calling me crazy?'

Frustration boiled on Hayter's face and he threw his mug to the side.

'I know painful ways to make people talk, and you WILL talk!'

He turned quickly and went over to Bunty's cases.

'This yours? Well, let's see what's in here.' He kicked it open and grabbed at a pile of clothes. 'You won't be needing this!' He heaped the garments onto the campfire.

Bunty simply glared back at him. But inside she was awash with worry.

The hunters' numbers swelled during the day: new faces arrived riding kylosaurs laden with empty cages. Bishop and Ash directed them to their tasks and the mood in the camp was celebratory . . . except for Christian Hayter. He had torn apart everything of Bunty's and not found a single clue that might help him. Furthermore, burning it all did not achieve the desired effect. 'Everything is replaceable,' Bunty had commented although she had become concerned when Hayter emptied her handbag. For a moment she thought he would find her ribbon-bound sack of letters but was somewhat relieved when she realised they were missing. Where were they?

'If you don't want to talk, that's fine by me. We're moving this bumper catch back to town first thing in the morning to join the others on the next shipment.'

'I thought you did not trade in shadow raptors, Mr Hayter?'

'Got to fill my quota, and someone's been upsetting trade. Besides, the Beast, my pet tyrant, needs someone new to play with.' He leant in close to Bunty and laughed. 'Hicks and Hudson –' he pointed at the two closest men –

'put her in a cage like the others. She loves visiting saurs and there's one on this island she's not met yet.'

✦ ✦ ✦

The evening grew dark quickly and the dense jungle seemed to close in around the clearing. Before the moon could rise the camp was lit with the orange flicker of lanterns that circled the central fire. Bunty was thankful to still be wearing her coat but it was now damp from the day's heavy downpour. The fact that she was cramped up in a cage did not stop exhaustion getting the better of her and within an hour she had drifted off to sleep.

Bunty was jolted awake by the raptors in the cage next to her thrashing about, alarmed. The hunters, however, seemed unaware of any danger, and one got up and staggered almost out of sight, just letting a flicker of light dance over him as he relieved himself next to a tree. Suddenly there was a blood-chilling cry.

The hunter by the tree was screaming for his life and holding his hands to his chest. Before any of his friends could jump up the man was pulled back into the forest and silenced. Panic broke out in seconds as all scrambled to their feet and armed themselves, shouting wildly, before Hayter snapped some order into everyone.

'Shut it, stand still! I said SHUT IT!'

Silence fell on the clearing, apart from the hiss of the fire as a wet log fizzled.

'It was Kane, boss,' someone said. This was met with a

forceful *'shhhhhhhh'* from Hayter.

Then came a chilling delayed echo. *Shhhhhhhhhh.* It made the hairs on the backs of everyone's necks stand up. Bunty blinked and looked at the raptor next to her that was now motionless.

Shhhh uuuuuuutttt ittttt. The strange sound rang out again.

'Kane, is that you? Kane? Answer me!' Hayter called out. 'Stop messing about! You're all being tricked, you drunk fools.' Hayter lowered his gun and pointed to Kane who was re-emerging from the treeline. As he got closer and the dancing lanterns flickered over him it was clear that Kane was covered in blood. As he slumped to the ground the blackness called out to them all again.

Fooooollllssssssssss!

Hayter readied his aim and spun around. 'Show yourselves, you cowards!'

Co-o-wwerrrddddsssss, the woods echoed eerily back.

The men who weren't frozen with fear bolted, but their screams were cut short as soon as they left the glow of the fire.

'Stand your ground, men.'

'Boss, is it the ghosts you were shooting at earlier? Have they come back?' Ash backed up to Hayter, gun held high.

Ghhhhooooosssstttttssss. The jungle shivered back its answer. Ash's eyes rolled back as he fainted on the spot.

Something startled the kylos and they started groaning

and stamping. One of them knocked over two lanterns that crashed to the ground behind Hayter, so that he spun around in fright. The kerosine ignited in a plume of flames that billowed up into the air and illuminated a small, feathered figure.

'The raptor boy!' Hayter screamed, but the flames lasted only an instant and he was gone. 'Shoot, men, it's a raptor attack!'

But before a shot could be fired several black masses moved in on the startled men and took them down screaming. Hayter jumped to where the boy had been, straining his eyes in the darkness to see any sign of him. Then something landed on his back and dug its claws in deep.

Bunty looked at the carnage before her. Silhouetted figures fought hand to claw; gunshots rang out in all directions. One hunter ran up towards the cages but was snatched from the path with a terrible wail. The cacophony of screams was incredible.

Then, as if by divine intervention, the moon clipped the treetops and shone down onto the edge of the clearing. The vale of shadows illuminated, floodlighting Hayter with the feathered boy clamped to his back. Bishop, who was closest, seized the moment and whacked the boy hard with the butt of his freshly emptied rifle. But the boy clung on.

'Stand still, boss, I got this!'

Grabbing the barrel of the rifle he swung again, managing to take both Hayter and the boy down to the ground.

Hayter sprang to his feet, pulled out his bullhook and wielded it high over the boy, who attempted to shield himself with a wing. Hayter stamped on the boy's chest so that he let out a high-pitched cry of distress.

'Make them leave.' Hayter held the deadly hook threateningly above him.

The boy did nothing.

Hayter pushed down harder with his boot and the boy yelped again. All the shadow raptors stopped and looked at each other.

'MAKE THEM LEAVE.'

The boy had no idea what Hayter was saying but he knew his intentions and he made a long clicking noise like a cicada that started loudly and faded down to an inaudible hum.

The shadow raptors stepped back and melted into the trees and Bunty closed her tear-filled eyes.

'Lance Bishop, you have bagged yourself a bonus. Cage this filthy raptor boy.'

18

Let Me Tell You a Story

~ and a lot of listening ~

At first light Bunty's cage was strapped to the back of a kylos along with the other captured raptors. The morning light revealed just how deadly shadow raptors can be. Men were torn in half, disembowelled and mutilated beyond recognition. There were six corpses and only one was a shadow raptor. It was no surprise the mood in the camp was sombre.

Hayter strolled over with another two mugs of hot tea and stood in front of Bunty's cage. He said nothing, just gestured to two men to load the last cage next to hers. It contained the raptor boy, huddling in a mess of feathers deep in a corner. Bunty glared back at Hayter who did not blink once, just stood still and sipped away at his morning brew. When the men finished securing the cage Hayter stepped closer and held out the second tin mug of tea. Bunty was already broken, but she was not about to start the day drinking his tea again so she just clung onto the bars, motionless. Hayter, frustrated by her silence, reacted the only way he knew how and tossed the cup aside, letting the tea arc through the air and hit the ground, the mug landing further away with a *tonk* and a surprised shout from the unlucky recipient.

'Maybe you will have better luck talking to that than I did.' He pointed to the boy's cage. 'Perhaps he needs a lady's touch? A shoulder to cry on? A hot-water bottle for bedtime? Hopefully I've kicked in enough manners and respect.'

'You're not human,' Bunty replied.

'Interesting,' Hayter looked about his person. 'I don't have a red face, claws or feathers.' He mimed holding onto cage bars in front of him, 'Or a cage around me.'

Bunty removed her hands from the bars.

'Tell me what he knows and you will walk free.'

'Liar.'

'Tell me what he is and I will put you on the first boat off this island.'

'LIAR!' Bunty was not playing along.

'Tell me everything or you will both be tomorrow's breakfast for the Beast.'

Hayter turned and whistled to the front of the procession, gesturing for them all to move out. Within a moment the kylos lunged forward. He began to walk away.

Bunty stared back at Hayter as long as he was in sight and then turned to see two cold blue eyes boring into her. Bunty and the boy looked at each other, soaking in every feature of the person in front of them. To break the deadlock, Bunty quickly raised her eyebrows, flaring her eyes wide. The boy returned the gesture, opening his just as wide. Bunty then squinted back at the boy and to her joy he squinted back. Sticking out her tongue got the same reaction, as did the twitch of her nose. Eventually Bunty smiled softly and gently raised a hand to him. Tentatively, the raptor boy leant forward a little, intoxicated by this curious human's charm, his nostrils quivering as he breathed in her scent. He reached out a grubby paw and stroked her hand gently, tracing the bones beneath the skin, comparing them to his own. The kylosaur suddenly gave a shrug, rearranging its burden slightly and banging their cages closer together.

'There's no point me asking the many questions I have for you, is there? You can't talk, can you?' Bunty said.

He stared back at her, watching the sounds come out of her mouth and then tried to mimic her the best he could.

'Caan't taaalk caan you.'

Bunty smiled. 'Not bad, it even sounds a bit like me. I guess you'll have to do a lot of the listening then.' She squeezed his hand. 'Let me tell you a story.'

'My husband Sidney and I left England to go to America with Grace, my daughter, when she was only nine. We took Theodore with us to tend the saurs. There, much later, when Grace was sixteen, she met an American man

called Franklin. Such a handsome man, full of life
. . . you should have seen his family's ranch in California.
Franklin and his brother Cash were quite the showmen,
I can tell you. The tricks they got up to with Theodore!
Franklin and Grace fell in love. We returned to England
as war in Europe was brewing and Sidney had the family
business to look after. Grace was so happy then, returning
with Franklin on her arm, a slight American twang over
her English accent.' Bunty paused, remembering happier
times.

'Franklin and Grace married, and she moved out.
Then Sidney fell ill and in no time it was just the three
of us in the big house: Sidney, Theodore and I. Theodore
loved Sidney. Looked up to him, that boy did. Not like
a dog to its master, more than that, and Sidney knew it.
Theo had something, something untouched. An energy.'

Bunty stopped. The realisation that she did not know
where any of her loved ones were was too much to bear.
She dipped her hand into her coat pocket and pulled out
the Blue Horned Raptor of Paradise feather. With it came
the lost bundle of letters that Bea had carefully replaced. A
tear rolled down Bunty's cheek as she gasped in surprise.

The boy blinked. Poking his finger through the
cage he touched the female human's face and lifted off a
tear that he took back to his lips. It tasted just like his.
Why was she chirping away at him, why had the sounds
hurt her? He looked into her hands and saw the letters.

Placing a hand on hers he removed the top letter and held it up to her face and wiped away the tears with it. Bunty was too broken to do much more than lean forward and through the bars they hugged, her tear-soaked cheek pressed against his.

Holding the female human seemed so natural, but the boy had never done anything like this before. Humans were wild vicious animals who preyed upon his clan and other creatures. They trapped, snared and killed. Yet here was an alpha female who smelled of wild flowers embracing him: a touch without violence. The kylos jolted again and shook the moment away from them.

Bunty recoiled back within her cage. Emotions were not part of her demeanour, even in the jungle, so she composed herself.

'Thank you, please forgive me. It's been a long morning and eleven years of searching and waiting and worry.'

The boy let Bunty take the tear-soaked letter from his hands. He looked back at her with his electrifying eyes.

Bunty pulled herself together. 'I'm Barbara Ann Brownlee.' She held out her hand, then, rather than waiting for his agreement, took the boy's hand in her own and shook it. 'Very pleased to meet you. Tell me, I'm famished, is there a buffet car on this train?' She tried a small joke to lighten the situation.

He looked on in silence; she let go of his hand.

'Carter on this traiiin,' he replied.

Bunty broke out in a smile that in turn broke out more tears.

'Forgive me, child. If only I knew your name.'

Despite the one-way nature of the conversation, she decided to carry on with a brave smile.

'Where was I? Ah, Gracie and Franklin, they decided to go to Australia. For reasons I will never know they upped and left, just like that.' Bunty raised her eyebrows with a look of bewilderment. 'Beatrice, their daughter – the girl you met . . .' At the thought of her granddaughter Bunty broke down again. 'Oh, Bea! Where, what has become of you?'

Bunty sank her hands in her head and let out a sob that even the porter riding the kylos heard.

The boy took the female human's hand again and squeezed it tight.

Bunty continued.

'Beatrice, bless her soul, had scarlet fever and Grace was not happy to leave without her, but she did – and that was the last we saw of them.'

Bunty looked back into the boy's cold blue eyes, then down at the letter.

'And then this arrived, out of the blue, eleven years late. I came looking for answers but I've just found you and this one feather!' Bunty breathed in deeply. 'All this terrible business with these brutes, and it's probably all my fault. Theodore's shot, Beatrice won't last out in the jungle on her own and we're to be breakfast for Hayter's Beast.'

Bunty lifted the letter to her face and sank into it.

The boy pulled it away and smiled; there was nothing else he knew to do.

'You know, I trust this will never be repeated, but . . . your eyes. Your eyes are the same as Franklin's.'

Bunty held the boy's face through the bars.

The moment lasted years. The kylos rocked back and forth along the path, thumping the ground with every footstep.

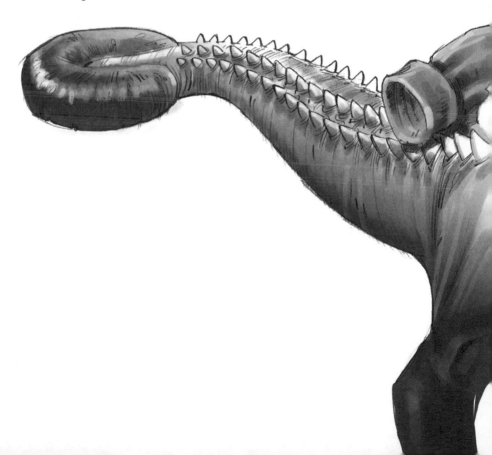

19

The Bigger You Are, The Harder You Fall

~ who's that girl? ~

From his cage next to Bunty, the raptor boy couldn't see much. The pair of them had been jostled and bounced into a stupor by the kylos's motion on the long trek, but the one thing he could see was the sky. Black clouds were ominous and heavy with rain. He knew this was going to be quite some storm; the air was already static with electricity.

Hayter was not known for being flexible with his schedule – and right now the only thing he could think of was getting his cargo back to town. His men knew the rain was coming, but they would rather get wet than mess with the boss. A man trotted past the boy's cage, his mimus bobbing in fear as it turned its head sideways to eye the clouds above the tree canopy. It sensed something else too, a feeling in the air. The boy gently reached a hand through the bars and tapped Bunty awake. She looked around the cramped cage groggily, rolling the stiffness out of her neck, rubbing her face. The moment Bunty stirred, the rain started.

These weren't raindrops like you might know them. These were great, fat heavy things that bounced when they hit the earth and hammered the upturned leaves like a billion drums being beaten at once. There was nothing gradual or gentle about this rain; it was the sort you have to shout to make yourself heard above, and within seconds everything is drenched. In less than a minute the path around the men and saurs had become ankle-deep in slick mud. For the kylos, slippery mud can be deadly. There's a phrase 'The bigger you are, the harder you fall.' A two-ton kylos falls pretty hard.

A gang of three hunters trotted past the cage on smaller and more ragged mimusaurs, water pouring off their hats, eyes squinting against the deluge. A huge crack of thunder split the sky. And then there was another, unexpected noise – a long, tearing, splintering followed by a loud crack and yells of warning. The two prisoners looked at each other, eyes wide, as branches along the path seemed to shake and sway, adding to the cacophony. One skittish mimusaur had become startled and slipped over, bringing the procession of men and saurs to a complete halt.

Above the noise of the rain they could just hear a saur cantering up from behind them, sploshing through the sticky mud. It was Hayter, riding to the front with a grim look on his face, wrenching hard on his reins, knuckles

white with barely suppressed anger. He didn't shout, but somehow his low, menacing tone travelled clearly over the rushing noise of the rainwater.

'It's just a rotten old tree falling, you idiots. Happens all the time. You two – and you – look lively. Chop it and move it.'

A man ran past the cages holding a long, thick coil of rope. Then:

'Come on, hurry up! It's a tree not a rock. Fasten on to the kylos and pull those bits clear of the trail. I'll watch over our catch.'

The steady sound of axes and machetes biting into wood seemed to calm the men and saurs, happier now they all had a job to do. Hayter, not one to get his hands dirty without reason, sauntered over to the cage, water running down his face like tears. He wasn't crying, though. He just looked at Bunty.

Bunty looked right back and said, 'I'm not afraid of you.'

The downpour was loud, but Hayter heard. He came closer to the cage, his face right up against the bars. 'You should be. He said anything of interest yet?'

'Don't be ridiculous, you horrid little man. The boy's mute.'

Just as Bunty folded her arms and continued to stare at him, a second thunderous crack rang out, followed an instant later by a third. Then more screams. The kylos carrying Bunty and the boy snorted in alarm and swung round – just in time to see a group of five or ten panicked hunters dive into the bushes as a huge tree trunk slammed to the path.

Then, just as suddenly, the hunters were sprinting back onto the path, eyes wide with fear. Hayter unslung his rifle with a yell and looked for a target. 'What is it, lads?' he yelled, heading away from the cages and towards his men. 'What's going on?'

As they got closer, the reason for their terror became clear. They were pierced all over with small arrows and blow darts. Unlike bullets that stop a man instantly, poisoned missiles take a moment for their venom to reach the nervous system. One by one, the men's legs seemed to turn to rubber underneath them and they fell, jerking and twitching on the wet ground.

The boy was quick to spot the opportunity. He hooked a hand through the cage and, using one of his claw talons, flicked the latch open. He thrust his way out and covered Bunty's cage with his body, fanning out the feathers under his arms to protect her.

From between a gap in the bars and the boy's cloak of feathers Bunty could see Hayter, on foot, turning frantically on the spot, sighting down his rifle as he looked for a target, any target. With a vicious whistle an arrow slapped into the wooden stock of his gun just in front of his face, kicking up a mean splinter that slashed into his

cheek. His gun dropped from his numb fingers.

With the other hunters down and Hayter standing, pale-faced, hands in the air, Bunty and the boy's rescuers stepped into view. It was Kunava and his fellow tribesmen, joking and grinning from ear to ear, patting each other on the shoulders and waving at someone else where the fallen tree lay. Then, weary and bandaged but still standing, with spiked-up hair and just as broad a smile across a face covered in matching tribal warpaint, Theodore took his place amongst the warriors.

'Hello, Bunty, old girl. Looks like we arrived just in time!'

'Oh, Theodore!' Bunty gasped in amazement. 'I thought you were –'

'Dead? Not quite. Had a spot of bother with some wasps but I'm back on my feet now,' he said as he helped her down from the cage that the raptor boy had managed to open.

'Our friend here came and gave these rotters a good thrashing last night.' Bunty looked over gratefully to the boy.

'Be an angel and stand over there with the lad and our new friend Kunava. I've got something to sort out,' said Theodore. With that, he took a step towards Hayter, raised his fists in classic boxer's stance and said, 'Right then, chum, now you've lost your gun and your mates, let's see what you're really made of.'

'Fine by me, "chum",' replied Hayter, licking his lips and rolling his shoulders.

The problem was – as Hayter could see all too well – that while Theodore had recovered amazingly quickly, he was still clearly protecting his wounded shoulder. And Hayter had no qualms about exploiting a situation like this. As a fighter raised in the raptor pits of London's East End, his first move was instinctive. Instead of raising his fists to box, Hayter took one quick step forward, grabbed Theodore's bad arm and yanked on it, hard, before thumping a clenched fist right into the fresh wound.

Theodore buckled in pain and fell to his knees and Hayter, still holding his wrist, swung around him, locking Theodore's arm up behind his back and then wrapping his other arm around Theodore's neck. It was a brutal, unfair move, but fights like this aren't games. Hayter had learnt his trade the hard way.

What usually follows is that the victor slowly chokes his victim, using their body as a human shield. In this case, however, Fate lent a helping hand. Just as Hayter was twisting Theodore's arm, one of the kylos spotted a particularly juicy tree fern and lifted its front feet to reach it, swinging its huge, clubbed tail like a pendulum for balance. Hayter took the full brunt across his back and was flung several yards away, where he landed face down in a puddle at Bunty's feet.

Theodore fell face forward too and rolled over to discover, much to his bewilderment, that his opponent had simply disappeared. His decision to stay lying down was proved right as the huge saur's tail whistled back again, missing his face by inches.

Hayter rolled to his feet, teeth bared, glaring at Bunty and cocking his fist back to punch her, meaning to knock her down and use her as hostage. But leaping in front of Bunty the raptor boy opened out his arms so that his feathers splayed and hissed at Hayter.

Hayter unclipped his bullhook from his belt. 'I will break you like I do all the other saurs, boy.'

'It's over, Hayter.' Bunty dropped her hands onto the boy's shoulders. 'Put your stick away.'

But just outside everyone's view, unnoticed so far, was Bea – and Bea had in her hand an unused blow dart that had gone wide of its mark and landed on the spot where she now stood.

She took one look at Hayter, clutched the dart in her fist and drove it as hard as she could into the big man's left buttock.

'Ouch!' yelled Hayter, who turned on his heel and faced Bea. 'Who's that girl?'

He raised his arm high but before he could do anything Kunava's men peppered him all over with more of their blow darts. His legs went wobbly beneath him. As he collapsed to his knees his grip loosened and the bullhook fell out of his hand, dropping first onto his head then to the floor with a thump. Everyone watched the poison take over Hayter, whose eyes had rolled back. Finishing what she had started, Bea prodded Hayter, toppling him face down into the mud.

20

Sweet Dreams

~ he's special, that boy ~

Bea held on tighter than ever to her grandmother. The day's ordeals had cracked her tough exterior and she was very glad to scrunch her eyes shut and bury her head into Bunty, who softly patted her.

'I'm sorry for being mean to you,' Bea whispered.

'No. I'm sorry for bringing you here, Beatrice, please forgive me. I've lost too much in my life to lose you as well. Utterly foolish of me to put you into harm's way.'

The strange boy watched them.

Theodore gave them space before formally introducing Kunava in a manner that brought a little formality to the very wet clearing. 'Barbara Ann Brownlee, may I have the pleasure to introduce you to my new dear friend, Mr Kunava, leader . . .'

'Guardian.' Kunava chirped a correction.

'Guardian of the . . . what's your tribe's name, old boy?'

'Long ago we were the Saurman, you can call us that if you wish.'

Theodore froze, staring at Kunava until he regained his thoughts and broke the silence. 'Blimey – Saurman, you say. Well, well . . . er . . .'

'Ever so pleased to meet you.' Bunty quickly held out her hand to end the formalities before Theodore made more of a fool of himself.

Kunava realised she was offering to shake his hand and, not wanting to offend, quickly unstrapped and removed his homemade raptor-clawed glove and gave her hand the best shake he could manage. His red smile widened. 'Pleasure to meet with you.'

Bunty immediately realised something was at odds. The firm handshake she was expecting turned out to be weak, with no grip. Bea, at eye level, saw what the issue was. Kunava's right hand was small and pale, with spindly fingers more like a child's than a grown man's.

'Forgive my hand, it's not grown back that well. The raptor claws make up for my weakness.'

'Oh my, pardon me.' Bunty politely excused herself from his grip, but Bea was too curious to let this moment go without an explanation.

'What happened to it?'

Kunava held out his hand, stretching the small fingers, and Bea curiously stroked his soft palm. 'This new hand will get older and stronger with time. His boss –' he gestured to Hayter – 'a very nasty man, cut off my old hand some time ago.'

'It's grown back?' Bea asked.

'Don't be silly, Beatrice, Kunava is teasing you. Now why don't you help unstrap all the baggage from the kylos? Is that brightly painted one not our friend Junior?'

Bea looked over and, indeed, there was Junior laden with all the hunters' camping equipment.

'You can't lose your kylos on your first week working as a porter – what will your boss Sammy say?' Bunty winked at Bea and readjusted the raptor feather in her hair.

Bea smiled back. Her grandmother was starting to treat her a bit more like an adult and being given some responsibility felt like good distraction from the rain.

Theodore stepped in and rubbed his chin, contemplating something. 'Bea, my girl, can you keep an eye on the boy for me? We need to get a move on, so don't waste time untying the cages.' He unclipped his large knife, pulled it from its sheath and handed it to her. 'Cut the cages free, but don't cut your fingers off. Yours won't grow back like Kunava's.'

Theodore grinned at Bea to get some recognition for his joke but she gave him the usual eye-roll that accompanied all his bad jokes.

But for Bea this was in fact a big moment. Some things were so off-limits that she never even asked, and Theodore's knife was one of them. It was heavier than she expected and the blade was warm from being kept next to Theodore's side all its life.

Kunava's fellow tribes-
men were finishing off securing
Hayter's men, carefully removing
all the good darts that stuck out
from them to be used again. The mimus
had run off and the raptor boy kept his
distance for a while, observing everyone. As soon as
Bea went over to the kylos he moved over to her.

'You can help if you want,' she told him. She gestured
with Theodore's blade over to the other side of Junior but
he just stared at the knife.

'I don't think he'll let you use it, you're too young.' Bea
assumed her new higher ranking immediately, but, not
understanding anything she was saying, the boy reached
out and touched the blade just as Bea sliced through a
thick rope, nicking his finger.

'Careful, look what you've done!'

Bea quickly glanced back at Theodore, who was still
chatting with Bunty and Kunava and thankfully had not

seen. The boy looked at his bleeding finger but did not react to any pain, just popped it in his mouth and sucked on it. Then he reached out with his other hand and swiped the knife from Bea, this time holding the flat edge of the blade.

'Give it back,' Bea insisted quietly so as not to alert the adults.

The boy turned his body away from Bea and stared into the shining steel at his reflection. He took his finger out of his mouth and slowly touched his own face. Bea saw that his finger was no longer bleeding nor even leaving any trace of blood. He looked up at her, handed back the knife, and smiled.

'Thank you. Now, if you don't mind, we have work to do.'

The hunters tied up, Kunava called Bunty and Theodore over.

'You have to leave this island, and quickly.'

'How long have we got?' Theodore asked.

'Tip-toed tree-frog poison is fast-acting but the effects only last a few hours. My men will tie the hunters to the trees, to give you more time, and put sticks in their mouths so they don't swallow or chew their tongues while they're out of it.'

'Remind me why we're bothered about that?' said Theodore as he dragged Hayter over to where his other men had fallen.

'If we stooped as low as them we would be no better than them.' Bunty opened her umbrella that she had retrieved from the cage, but it was no use – she was already wet to the skin. 'But I will allow you that punch on the nose you owe that terrible man for hurting that raptor back at the depot.'

'No, Bunty, you're right – I'm better than that,' Theodore said, dropping Hayter to the floor in another puddle before leaning him up against a tree and thrusting a muddy moss-covered stick into his mouth. 'Open up now, there's a good boy. We don't want you hurting yourself, do we?'

'Someone will hear them. After their sweet dreams they'll probably wake up screaming. It's not a kind poison to humans.' Kunava chuckled to himself. 'But I suggest you get off the island pretty sharpish – you probably have until sunset tomorrow before Hayter gets back to town. And the saur boy has now been seen and he's made enemies – it won't be safe for him or the shadow raptors while he's on the island.'

'Can't the boy go and live with your tribe?' Bunty asked Kunava.

'My tribe? Oh no, lady, he's your tribe's problem now, not mine.'

'I don't understand – you called him a saur boy, so is he not one of the Saurmen, like you?'

Theodore stopped standing on Hayter's hand and moved over to listen.

'I believe that boy's parents came from another tribe of the Saurmen, far from here,' Kunava said. 'They were killed and he was taken and raised by the shadow raptors.'

They all turned and looked at the boy, who was now standing on top of a kylos laden with cages, trying to unravel the web of rope that held them in place. His wet feathers were not at their best.

'He's been in the jungle all his life?' Bunty asked.

'Yes. I keep an eye on him, follow his prints every now and then. He's been well looked after by the clan.'

'I can't possibly imagine what his life is like.' Bunty tried to understand the situation. 'But why do I have to look after him?'

'Not you, lady, you're not a Saurman. Theodore, you have to look after him.'

'Hang on, old chap. I'm not a Saurman either and I . . .'

'You sure about that?' Kunava cut in.

'Quite sure. Apart from not being a Saurman, I'm definitely not in a position to look after anyone. I can barely look after myself.' Theodore looked at Bunty and widened his eyes.

'Then how did you find the sacred tree, the one that grew from the temple?' Kunava asked.

Bunty and Theodore looked at each other again with puzzled expressions.

'What tree? What temple?'

'The tree where you met the saur boy and the shadow raptors. That raptor clan are the temple guardians. You don't just walk up to a temple, you need to have a key bone, and you have to be a Saurman to have a key bone.'

Bunty and Theodore heard the words but could make no sense of what the tribesman was saying.

Theodore turned to Kunava, who was strapping his claw glove back on. 'Sorry, old chap, I have no idea what you are on about.'

'Yes, you do. Take a look at my key bone.' Kunava parted the decorative feathers across his shoulders and removed a beaded necklace that hung over his chest. Set on a piece of grubby, hand-stitched leather was an odd-looking stone, about the size and shape of a carnivore's tooth. He prised open the metal clasps that kept it in place and held it up. As he did so, a drop of rain hit it and the stone sparked into life with dazzling speckles of colour.

'Gosh, that is beautiful! What type of stone is that?' Bunty enquired.

'It's actually a dinosaur bone that has turned to stone. But you know that, don't you, Mr Logan?' Kunava looked at a wide-eyed Theodore and handed him the key bone.

'Theodore, Theo . . . please end these tall stories and riddles; explain to Kunava that we don't know what he is on about and can't look after the boy. He simply won't fit in. His home is the jungle.'

Theodore could not take his gaze from the key bone; it was hypnotic. It was a very dark and dense blue with an almost dusty, matt finish to it. It had no reflection. But as he turned it in his fingers and the sunlight hit it, an iridescent sparkle lit up and travelled around the stone, moving through every colour in the rainbow.

'Amazing, truly amazing . . .' he muttered.

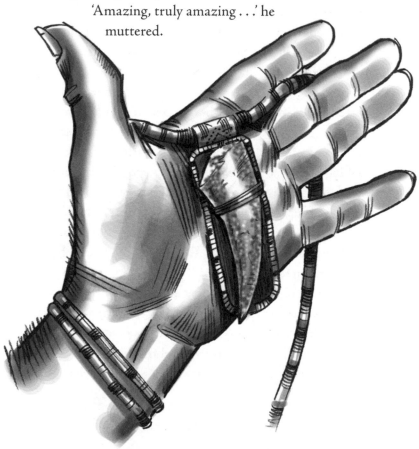

Bunty broke the spell. 'Theodore, give it back.'

Theodore looked at Bunty and back to Kunava, weighing up in his mind what he should say, and, more to the point – what he should not say.

'Sorry, old chap. I honestly don't know anything about dinosaur bones. But . . .' He looked at Bunty and paused. 'I will take the boy from this island.'

Kunava's smile returned wider than ever and he took the key bone from Theodore and popped it back in its setting. 'You know he's special, that boy, don't you? His time as a supersaur has finished, he has now to become human. You need to teach him.' Pleased with the outcome, Kunava trotted off to his men who were now, with the boy and Bea's help, releasing all the trapped animals, birds and Raptors of Paradise back into the jungle.

Bunty, who had remained silent but with a screwed-up expression all over her face, turned to Theodore. 'What on earth are you doing? We can't take him with us!' she blurted out.

Theodore turned to her. 'May I remind you, Bunty, that you took in a stray boy once, and he didn't turn out to be that bad. Perhaps I am meant to look after him?'

'Don't be silly. You weren't raised by raptors, nor do you have a glitter-covered rock.'

'When I was young, the only love and care I had growing up was from saurs,' Theodore replied. 'My father barely looked at me, everyone blamed me for my mother's death when I was born – if Lady and Champion had not licked me clean and fed me scraps from the saurmonger's floor I probably would have never survived. But I did.'

Bunty had no reply; she knew Theodore was speaking the truth.

'And it's not a glitter-covered rock, it's a 150-million-year-old opalised prehistoric dinosaur bone, probably originally from the lightning field opal mines of South Australia. But, more to the point,' said Theodore, 'we need to get Junior back to the Old Town and get ourselves aboard the *Orca* – and quickly. Kunava's right, this place has just become a lot more dangerous.'

Bunty could see that Theodore knew more than he was letting on; this extra information confirmed it. She also knew not to press him. At some point he would find the right moment to explain this.

Bunty gathered their things together as Theodore and Bea started releasing the last of the captured raptors.

The rain and the thunderous noises stopped as suddenly as they had started. The dark gloom lifted and streaks of hot sunshine burned holes in the canopy above them.

Kunava signalled to his men that it was time to get going, but not before helping themselves to most of Hayter's supplies and equipment, which was loaded onto the two prickleback kylosaurs. Kunava paused for a while, waiting to catch the saur boy's eye. He was distracted and smelling the air. Kunava *tooooted* the high-pitched call of a Golden Fantailed Raptor, and at that the saur boy immediately looked round. The two had never actually met but they had observed each other many times over the years. Kunava slowly walked over and bent down so that they were eye to eye. He placed a hand on the boy's shoulder and stared at him deeply. In the moments that followed no words passed between them, just a mutual understanding of sorts. Kunava could see the many questions in the boy's head. In return Kunava had a wealth of information that he knew the boy needed to know but had no words that he would understand. One day they would meet again and be able to converse, but for now he just smiled back at him.

Theodore also felt the need to ask more questions of the tribesman and came over.

'Kunava, I want to show you something.'

'I saw it: you set it into the handle of your knife. Don't worry, your secret is safe with me. I'm just the crazy half-handed man you met in a jungle.'

'Honestly, old boy, I was given that stone.'

Kunava paused. 'And how do you think I got mine?'

'But I didn't know it was a key, or what it unlocks.'

'You have just unlocked the rest of your life, my friend. Keep the saur boy safe. He's special, that boy, very special.'

With that, Kunava turned and disappeared into the thick dense green of the jungle.

21

The Rainbow Shakedown

~ you won't see that in a guide book ~

The boy stood in a shard of light that had penetrated the dense canopy and spotlighted the jungle floor. The humans were squawking at each other about something. His growing curiosity in them would have to wait, he had other important things to do. The feathers that he had bound along his arms and ankles needed to be dried, sorted and groomed. A routine he had done every day since he acquired them.

Grooming always took place after each day's downpour of monsoon rain. Normality could not resume unless the clan was in pristine condition. Out of all the saurs in the world, the variety of raptors who lived in these remote islands were the most concerned with maintaining their good looks. It was this vanity that had evolved the Raptors of Paradise into the most colourful and flamboyant of their kind. The females' taste for perfection also demanded that the males became the best at courtship dancing, mimicking and maintaining their immaculate dance arenas, often with ornate and random items. Who could

build the best nest was basic in comparison: these raptors had to do a lot more to ensure their genes were passed on.

The boy methodically outstretched both arms and slowly rotated his wrists then his elbows, so that all the feathers fanned out. He held this position for a while, checking that all his plumage was in order. Then, in one swift movement, he raised his arms and quickly brought them together, clapping his hands at its climax. A fine spray of water flew across the jungle and, as the light caught every droplet a rainbow filled the clearing. Bea let out a gasp of delight at the spectacle.

Theodore, still working, opened the last and largest cage and out burst the two shadow raptors. Spotting their fellow clan member they ran straight to him, stretching their cramped legs. Each lowered their head in front of him and tilted it from side to side, looking up from their left and right eye in turn. They all stood just enough distance away from each other, then proceeded to give themselves a good shakedown. Not too dissimilar from a wet long-haired dog, they sent arcs of fine water droplets in every direction, lighting up the clearing with rainbow flashes.

'You won't see that in a guide book.' Theodore nudged Bea with his elbow as he strapped the last of Hayter's provisions onto Junior.

After rearranging his own feathers, the boy turned his attention to the larger raptor. Struggling in the cramped cage had dislodged many of its feathers. By combing the raptor's feathers back into position with his fingers some were saved, but many had to be plucked out. Discarding the badly broken ones, the boy held back a small handful that he stuffed into his waistband for later. He continued to comb over the area, pulling the raptor's surrounding feathers into the gaps and stopping to pluck the odd bug along the way, popping the juiciest ones into his mouth.

The boy could not remember when he worked out that he was not actually going to grow any feathers himself. At first he had looked like one of the bald featherless infants, but as they grew up and filled out around him he realised he was different. He joined in the grooming routine as best he could but ended up just helping the others. The boy started keeping the redundant feathers and eventually used them to create his own plumage, binding them with vine and cord to his limbs, in a system which, after a period of trial and error, he got to work for him. His up-close observations of the clan told him that their feathers were layered and he copied this on his own cloak, fashioned from feathers of every member of the clan. He developed his own adaptation of the shakedown that did not send his feathers flying and assimilated himself as best he could.

The smaller raptor had kept its watchful gaze over the humans and when it was his turn to be groomed the larger raptor took over staring down Bea and Bunty. The boy opened his mouth and croaked an unusual noise, to which the raptor responded immediately with the same sound. However, as it opened its mouth wide, the feathers surrounding its face flared out to reveal a shimmering scarlet halo of finer feathers underneath.

'Magnificent, simply magnificent!' Bunty nudged Bea with excitement. 'Quite spectacular they are, under their drab coats.'

'I guess they need to keep the colourful feathers hidden if they are to blend into the shadows,' Bea replied. 'They can't sneak up on their dinner waving that about.'

'Probably just brings them out for special occasions, I would imagine. Oh, what a treat to be seeing them in their full glory like this,' Bunty concluded.

The boy fanned out and removed old red feathers with his fingers, keeping the undamaged ones for himself. He had lost his own homemade headband of red feathers in the raid on Hayter's camp and would need to remake it. It had taken ages to perfect the layering so that he could manually flick forward the larger feathers that started behind his ears, with the rest of the headband following, mimicking the movement of his fellow raptors.

With one last croak of approval the grooming was over. Not ones for thank yous or goodbyes, the two raptors turned and within a flash had disappeared into the undergrowth. The boy stood quietly, raised his hands up, clenching his fists tightly and releasing them. Then he inhaled deeply and exhaled in a solemn huff. He would try to be more human for a while.

He slowly straightened his back from his stooped raptor position, raised his head high and stepped out of the shard of light. Mimicking a human's stance and gait, he walked over towards the others.

Bunty took a few paces forward and met him halfway.

'I think this is yours?' She held out the red-feathered headband that she had just retrieved from a pack strapped to a kylos. 'That ghastly Hayter had it.'

He stared at it and then back up at Bunty.

'Now, let's see if I can put this in for you, my boy. It's a fine set of feathers, some of the most beautiful I've ever seen and I'm sure if you were on Bond Street right now this little lot would set you back a fair penny. Quite the rage . . . but I think they are more suited here than in any city.' Bunty paused as the bizarreness of the situation dawned on her. The people buying these feathers had no idea from where and what they had come. Or, more to the point, the sadness, pain and death that the barbaric exotic feather trade caused.

She guided the headband past the boy's ears and slid it back over his forehead and onto his brow. 'Nonetheless, it's just as wet here as it is in London. Handsome, that you are, my boy, and this helps to keep the hair from your eyes. You've seen some sights, I am sure. Now, I'm probably going about this all wrong but let's have a go anyway.' She smiled deep into his eyes as she proceeded to push the feathers back into his slick matted hair.

'Quite a task. I expect it's well over a year – make that a couple of years – since you have had a bath . . . There you are. You look splendid, not a feather out of place . . . well, not that I can see.'

Bunty held him at arms' length and squinted, tilting her head to the left and right in the same manner as the raptors did.

The boy had never been groomed before, and it felt good. He knew that the headband was the wrong way round, but he did not see fit to correct it. The noises she made sounded good. Soft, rhythmical and like birdsong. Her delicate aroma filled the air around him; a complex mix of pollen and fauna followed her about like a shadow. He had to be brave; he had to trust her as returning to the clan was not safe. He lowered his gaze from Bunty so she would not see his eyes welling up.

'Wooooow! Get it off my foot!' cried out Theodore behind them.

The boy wiped his eyes and looked over to find Theodore struggling with Junior. He had managed to move the stubborn kylos, but it was now standing on his foot. The boy clicked a noise out of one cheek and, without any fuss, Junior lumbered over towards him. Theodore, relieved, hopped up and down and continued to curse the air for a while. Junior nuzzled his head into the boy's side as he patted it softly. With another clicking noise they moved off, back in the direction of the Old Town.

'Can we go home now, please, Grandma?' Bea tugged at Bunty's dress.

'Yes, my dear. This place is far too dangerous to stay.'

'And the boy?'

'He can't stay either. I don't know how to help, but for now, Theodore has offered to look after him.'

Bea looked up at her grandmother. 'Oh, that's wonderful, but Theodore can't even . . .'

'I know, quite out of his depth here and out of character too, but people can change. He made me a cup of tea once without burning it . . .'

Bea laughed, Bunty put her arm around her and they both followed, well behind Junior's happily swinging club tail.

Within minutes the clearing that had hosted so much activity was silent, except for the rhythmic snoring of Hayter and his men, slumped and tied to a tree.

On the trail, Theodore picked up the pace and jogged to the front, taking care not to put too much weight on his trodden foot and caught up with the boy.

'Thanks, lad.' Theodore's eyes were wide with respect as he came over. 'I guess that's two I owe you now, kid.' He rubbed his healing wound.

The boy looked up at him with a twinkle of a tear in his eye, then, in a little mock Cockney voice, said, 'Knees up, Mother Brown'.

22

A Creamy Milk Moustache

~ the tooth fairy doesn't come out this far ~

The procession was making its way back to the Old Town in good time. Junior instinctively knew the way back home and as the path got wider and they reached the main trail they were not having to cut back overhanging vines or remove obstacles that had fallen across the path. It was a great relief to arrive at Biggie's base camp knowing that the Old Town was only another half-day's trek, and that here they could offload all the confiscated kit and rations from Hayter and his men. This more than made up for Biggie's equipment that had been lost along the way and Theodore, with the help of Bea, hid it all with the rest of Biggie's stash. From the look of it the boy knew his way around the camp well: he went straight for the hidden water barrels and knew exactly where the cups were, filling one for everyone.

Bunty opened up the medical kit, dressed Theodore's wound and replaced the sling. She had learnt to do field dressings during the war and had nursed Theodore back to life after his return from the Front so this was second nature to her. Theodore thanked her and, returning the medical kit, saw the box of explosives.

'Think this might come in handy,' he muttered to himself as he carefully removed it and loaded it on Junior.

There was no time to make a campfire, but thankfully in Hayter's kit there was an abundance of SPAW and a loaf of bread that was not yet stale. Bea carefully opened up two tins with the small keys provided and made sandwiches for everyone. She had also found a short round tin with no label that she was hoping would be peach halves in syrup, her favourite. Unfortunately she discovered it was evaporated milk, her worst nightmare.

Bunty's eyes, however, lit up, and after everyone else passed on the sickly sweet milk, she happily had the whole tin to herself. 'I simply adore evaporated milk. My, what a luxury!'

The boy was repulsed by the liquid and looked rather baffled at the sandwich, opting to just eat the SPAW filling with his hands.

'Come on, lad, you need to keep your strength up. Try the bread.' Theodore winked at him. 'Found hundreds of these SPAW tins back at his nest,' he told Bunty. 'Looked like he'd acquired a few things over the years from the hunters.'

'I admire his survival skills, but I still can't quite believe he's been here all his life. I mean how on earth did he survive in the jungle as a baby? What did he eat?' Bunty was doing her best to elegantly eat her sandwich.

'Raptors regurgitate food to their young before they can feed themselves,' Theodore mentioned, swallowing down his last bite.

Bea spoke up. 'Don't many animals and birds do that?'

'True. My guess is that he was fed like that.'

Bunty looked up with a creamy milk moustache. 'I can't think of anything more ghastly, eating something that was supposed to feed another animal!'

Bea pointed and laughed out loud. 'What, like milk that comes from a cow?'

Theodore and the boy looked up too and the three of them fell about in hysterics.

The end was in sight. As they got closer to town, the boy's eyes grew wider and wider. Bea noticed that his head was turning more and more. This was clearly uncharted territory for him.

The boy had never walked amongst other humans, although he had watched from afar. Everything was totally new to him. When the trees finally parted and the sea was in sight he held back and waited at the treeline as the others staggered onto the beach, passing some stray Mittenhead hadros.

Bea had spied Sammy, who let out a cry of relief and

disbelief and ran straight over. Biggie, checking a fishing net strung between two shacks, turned and held his hands high with joy as Bunty and Theodore broke into a quick jog down the shore to meet him. Junior was thinking of nothing other than a cool refreshing dip in the sea and trudged into the shallows, still piled with kit bags, splashing his club tail back and forth.

Bea turned and saw the boy, alone.

'Sammy, you remember your ghost story, the one about the winged

spirits who live in the jungle?'

Sammy looked at Bea. 'You know that's just a story to get children to do as they are told, don't you?'

'Really? Well, anyway,' she beckoned to the boy.

Sammy looked up to see what she was waving at. His jaw dropped.

'A winged spirit!'

'Yes, he's going to stay with us,' Bea said. 'Theo is apparently going to look after him . . . but I have a good feeling I am going to be looking after the both of them.'

Her waving was doing nothing to entice him over so she grabbed Sammy's hand and dragged him up the beach to the treeline.

'Sammy, this is . . . er . . . well, he has no name, yet.'

'Pleased to meet you, Has-no-name-yet.' Sammy put out his hand.

The boy looked at it and tapped it with his to make it go away.

'Bea, why is he wearing shadow raptor feathers?'

'Strange, isn't it? He can't say a word either, just copies things – look.'

Eye to eye she faced the boy and slowly spoke so it would sink in. 'All the fun of the seaside.'

Sammy looked on and Bea kept her gaze on the boy for longer than was necessary, then repeated: 'All the fun of . . .'

'The seaside,' the boy replied in a perfect Bea voice.

Sammy pulled back and marvelled at the boy. 'Busy Bee, that was a very marvellous trick. Do it again.'

The boy jerked his head around, looked Sammy in the eye and said, in Sammy's voice, 'Marvellous trick, do it again.'

'Whooo! That's amazing. Now check this.'

Sammy pulled off his top, threw his cap in the air and ran back down the beach, his arms outstretched, and dived head-first into the sea next to Junior.

Bea turned and looked at the boy.

'Now, that's a challenge – come on!'

She pulled off her jacket, tossed it high into the air and, running at full pelt, screamed 'Arrrrrrrrrr!' as she launched into the sea with a huge splash.

The boy looked on and dipped his toes into the hot sand. He had only been in this place at night in the cool dark air. The end of the day glowed red; it was a very different place to be in. He looked about to make sure everything was safe. Every move that he had ever made in the jungle was considered and cautious. But there was nothing holding him back, so he un-bit his lip, let out a long scream 'Arrrrrrrrrrrr!' – and ran at full speed over the hot sand and into the sea where Sammy and Bea were splashing about.

✦ ✦ ✦

Everyone looked around at the sound of the children playing. Biggie swiftly introduced Bunty and Theodore to his wife, Jara. She smiled warmly, and when she saw that Theodore's arm was in a sling, insisted on dressing the wound for him. Bunty filled them in on the headline news about Hayter and their ordeal and, not knowing what to say about the boy, skirted around the exact details and just said that they had found him alone in the jungle. Jara looked over to the children splashing, then to Biggie with a puzzled expression.

'Bunty, you will have to explain this to me later, but first, let's get cooking. You must be all starving.' She let out a whistle and beckoned over to her son. 'Sammy, come now, dry yourselves off and then show your friends your room.'

+ + +

Sammy's room was barely large enough for his thin mattress that had been well patched over the years. Hanging from a few nails on the wall were a complete set of clothing, a single red boxing glove with something scribbled on it and a large poster for a saur circus that showed a stytop and an oviraptor performing a trick.

'I've been to one of those, you know.' Bea pointed to the poster.

Sammy's mouth dropped to the floor in awe. 'Seriously?'

'Tell you what, when I get home I'll send you some more posters like it with all the other saurs they have. It's the least I can do to thank you for everything.'

The boy was also mesmerised by the poster, and not fully understanding what it was he tapped it a few times and looked behind it. Next to it on the wall was a tattered postcard of the Statue of Liberty. Sammy handed it to Bea.

'Have you seen this lady before? Look how big she is!'

Bea smiled but did not want to spoil his imagination with the truth.

Sammy pulled up his mattress at the corner and took out a small box. He set it down and Bea joined him on the floor.

'This is my box of very important things,' Sammy told them. He pulled out a snow globe with a model of the Eiffel Tower inside it and gave it a shake. 'Look, snow!'

The boy was amazed and stared into it until every last flake settled and then shook it again.

Bea picked up a chipped magnifying glass and passed it to the boy who had no idea what to do with it until Sammy manoeuvred it in front of the boy's face. He leapt back when he saw the snow globe suddenly enlarge in front of him. Sammy pulled out a set of cigarette cards mostly depicting baseball players.

'This one here, he plays for the New York Yankees – look, we have the same cap.' Sammy flicked the visor of his moth-eaten hat and proudly smiled at both of them. He shuffled the cards and found another of interest.

'He is a boxer, I have been saving for a long time and soon I will be able to afford another glove.' He pointed at the single glove that hung from the wall with pride. 'And my father made this for me.' Sammy opened up a smaller box with shells stuck to the outside. In it was a rusty pen-knife, some coins from around the world and a tin soldier riding an allosaur.

'They are all wonderful, Sammy,' Bea said, but inside she was feeling guilty at the thought of her large bedroom at home, piled with every toy and gift she could ever want. As Sammy put away his possessions the boy reached into his feathered outfit and pulled out a small woven bundle. He held it out in two hands for them to observe, and smiled.

'Is that a weaver bird's nest?' Sammy pondered as the boy carefully unfolded a small opening at the top and tipped out the contents onto the floor in front of them. The boy looked up and proudly smiled at them both.

There was a bottle opener, a pair of bent spectacles with no glass, three marbles, a blue beer-bottle top, four coins, a queen of diamonds playing card, a broken button, a paper clip, a porcupine quill, two bullets, one of Bea's shells with a hole drilled in it and an old tobacco tin that now contained some small teeth. Bea pointed at the boy's mouth and back at the box and he tapped his adult front teeth and gave a big smile back.

'I guess the tooth fairy doesn't come out this far,' Bea smiled back.

23

A Few Years
Out of Fashion

~ smartest clothes on the island ~

'Tell me more about the boy?' Biggie pulled Theodore outside, gesturing to walk with him away from the others.

'I was hoping you might know, Biggie. We found him, or he found us.'

'Have you not asked him?'

'There's a language problem. He can mimic what we say but I don't think he has any idea *what* he is saying.'

'So he can't talk?'

'Well, he can squawk, he seems to know what the shadow raptors are saying. We met a Saurman called Kunava who told us the boy had been raised by shadow raptors.'

Biggie thought for a moment. 'Saurmen? Never heard of that tribe, are you sure? I once knew a Kunava, though, a good man, lived here in the Old Town. He used to do odd jobs and trade spice till he got his hand cut off.'

Theodore paused. 'This tribesman had a withered small hand that he kept hidden in a homemade claw glove.'

Biggie looked just as baffled as Theodore.

'Nope. Must be another Kunava. He definitely had his hand cut right off, saw his stump myself.'

Theodore thought for a moment before speaking, as he knew it sounded crazy, even to his own ears. 'He did mention that his hand was taking time to regrow.'

'Ha ha, he told you that – ha! Now are you sure Hayter didn't hit you over the head? Raised by raptors he said as well, that's also crazy talk. You spent five days in the jungle and only just survived, my friend – look at the state of you. A boy would not last a day.'

'What about his feathers, then?' Theodore asked.

'All the tribes in these islands wear feathers, have done for ever and ever. I admit that I have never seen them worn like that, but there are so many tribes dotted all over these islands. The boy could be from any one of them.'

'I saw his camp and there were raptor nests alongside it,' Theodore said stubbornly.

'Did you see him there with the raptors?'

'Yes, well, no – I can't be too sure. I was in and out of consciousness and in a great deal of pain whilst he was clawing at my wound. I passed out.'

'Sounds like it was a nightmare you were having. I've been all over the jungle, never seen a boy living there.'

'I think he's the one who's been pinching your kit. He

knew where all your stuff was hidden.'

'Or it could be your friend Kunava, it could have been him who clawed you better in his camp?'

Theodore sat down and shook his head.

'You have been shot and beaten. . .'

'And stung.'

'Come, come, have a drop of my rum and forget about this crazy talk.'

Theodore shrugged. 'Maybe you're right.'

'I know I am.' Biggie spun the top of the bottle and handed it to Theodore.

✦ ✦ ✦

While the men got stuck into the bottle the kids herded Junior back into his paddock. Sammy was happy to see his kylos and Bea again, but was not happy with the news that Christian Hayter had taken Junior, even though it was only for two days.

'This is not good for business, no way. Busy Bee, you should not have let him be taken. I told you to look after him.'

The boy was admiring the saur's paintwork and keeping his head down. Living with shadow raptors had taught him to blend in not stick out.

'I got him back, what's wrong?'

'I'll tell you what's wrong: Hayter!'

'We all know that, Sammy!' Bea tried to make light of her telling-off.

'No! Hayter has seen him, seen him with you – that means he knows I have helped you!'

Bea bit her lip. 'Sorry.'

'Sorry is not going to get me out of trouble when you jump off this island. We need to think of something, and fast.'

The boy had become more curious about the colouring on Junior's bony plates and scratched at it with one of his broken and chipped dirty nails until the paint came off. Bea saw this out of the corner of her eye and quickly stepped in, holding down his hand and waved a waggling finger with the other.

'No scratching the paintwork.' She tried as best she could to convey the message, but Sammy took notice.

'No, the saur boy is right.'

Bea looked back at him puzzled, as did the boy, who had no idea what was going on.

'We scratch off Junior's paintwork, all of it.'

Bea was looking puzzled still, so Sammy explained. 'Hayter and everyone on this island knows Junior, he's handsome and colourful. Take away his paintwork and he's just handsome, just like all the other kylos.'

'So Hayter won't recognise him!' Bea said.

'Correct. I will say Junior was stolen by a ruthless thirteen-year-old girl bandit who tricked me.'

'Go on . . .' Bea liked the sound of this plan.

'I had to dip into my life savings and get a new kylos.'

'Do you think it will work?' Bea asked.

'It has to. I've already told a few people down at the dock that . . .'

'That what?'

'That a ruthless thirteen-year-old girl bandit tricked me!'

'You said what? What else did you say?' She stamped her foot.

'Nothing, something about a drinking contest and then a game of cards that I bet on too heavily.'

'And?'

'And that's it, honest, no hanky-panky, just cold-hearted Busy Bee. The terrible ruthless and cunning trickster that stole my heart and my kylos.'

Bea uncrossed her hands and walked over to Junior. The boy looked away. Bea bent down and gave Sammy a kiss on the cheek.

'Sounds like a good plan. Let's put it into action.' And with that she did a Theodore, rallying her clans and issuing orders on who was to do what, making sure the boy was doing it properly.

◆ ◆ ◆

'It's hot, come and get it!'

Jara called everyone in and put some fish stew in bowls on the table. She was happy to have visitors even though she no longer had her favourite chair to rock away the evening in. Sammy had already received an earful when he had returned without the chair days earlier, but she knew people were more valuable than possessions. A contented silence fell over the hungry visitors as they ripped apart the fresh bread on the table and dived in with their spoons.

'My, this is delicious, Jara, thank you,' Bea got in quickly before Bunty.

'Is he not hungry?' Jara pointed to the boy who was staring at the steam rising from the bowl and curiously sniffing the hot vapours.

Bea picked up his spoon and placed it in his hands and helped him with the first dip into the stew, selecting a tasty lump of fish. Everyone looked on as the boy leant in and touched it with the tip of his tongue. Bea could see his mind whirling as his tastebuds fired up. Theodore gestured for him to pop it in his mouth and he cautiously placed the spoon in his mouth but instantly pulled it out and spurted soup over the table. Theodore was quick with his handkerchief and a good excuse.

'Sorry, that's my fault. I don't think he's ever had hot food or anything with such flavour before.'

Jara took a new plate and scooped the hot fish out onto it.

'There you go, let it cool down before you eat it.'

Jara's infectious loving smile spread out to everyone in the room.

'I guess he will have to do everything for the first time.'

◆ ◆ ◆

After dinner Bunty and Bea helped wash up the bowls.

'No need to do that, but thank you,' said Jara.

'It is us who need to thank you, Jara, and I'm terribly sorry for the loss of your lovely chair.'

'No worries, please.'

She looked the two of them up and down – Bunty in her ragged dress and Bea in her tattered clothes – and said, 'Come now, I have some spare clothes for you both.'

Bunty glanced at Jara who was tiny but with a huge bosom, and tried to gracefully decline.

'Honestly there is no need, besides I don't think your clothes would ever fit.'

'Oh no, I don't mean my clothes. I've been hanging onto these for ages with no one to give them to. You'd be perfect.'

Jara beckoned them inside, went over to the corner of the room and took a framed family photo and some other items off the top of a small upright trunk. She flipped the locks, opened it up and delved in, pulling out a wonderful pristine western-style white blouse.

'Here, my little lady, one for you. Go on, take it,'

She pulled out a second, more floral one, for Bunty.

'And one for you. Smartest clothes on the island, too

good for me, better you have them.'

Bea was amazed to be handed something so beautiful and clean. It was not what she would normally wear for escaping off an island but it was too good to turn down.

'Look at the fine detail.'

Bunty exclaimed. 'Oh, it's lovely, Jara, thank you.' She held it up and swirled around in it, sending the hem up in the air.

'Wherever did you get it?' Bea asked and looked inside the blouse to put it on. Suddenly all the colour drained from her face and she staggered forward, holding herself up on the edge of the table. Bunty turned and looked around at her.

'Beatrice, my love, are you all right? It looks like you've just seen a ghost!'

Theodore stepped into the room just as Bea passed out. He leant in and caught her before she fell.

'Bea! Whatever's happened?'

Bunty took the blouse from Bea's limp hands and looked at the name-tag sewn into it.

'Oh, my . . .' She held her hand to her mouth.

'What?' Theodore demanded.

'It . . . it . . . it's . . . Grace's.'

24

Ghosts of the Past

~ something is connecting us ~

'Jara, how did you come by these clothes?'

'A lovely lady called Gracie left them here for safekeeping a long time ago. I don't think she's coming back, so I thought you could have them.' Jara seemed a little bewildered.

'Grace Kingsley is my daughter – Bea's mother – we came here to . . .' Bunty looked at Bea, who was coming round in Theodore's arms. 'To try to find out what happened to her.'

'Gracie and that handsome husband of hers, Frankie?'

'So you knew them both?'

'Of course. They stayed here for a while, they loved my fish stew.'

'And what happened to them, where did they go?'

'Word went around that they had . . .' Jara looked at Bea who was now conscious and softly spoke the rest, 'that they were killed by raptors.'

Bunty lifted her hand to her mouth. It was the first time anyone had spoken out loud what she had feared.

Theodore looked gravely at Bunty.

'Bea, my love, how are you feeling? Are you up for hearing the truth?'

Bea nodded her head and pulled the blouse tightly to her face to see if she could smell her mother but nothing was there.

'Jara, tell me, Grace and Franklin, did they trek into the jungle alone?' Theodore asked.

'No, no, that's crazy, no one goes in alone. I think there were a group of them and a guide, but as I recall only two returned and they fled the island.'

Bunty swallowed and looked to the floor.

'Many people come here to see the Raptors of Paradise – only a few get to see them and only a few of them walk out alive. You are the lucky ones. I have known many that never returned, but Gracie and Frankie, that was tough. It hurt me deeply when I found out, especially with the baby boy, it makes the story all the more sad.'

Bunty and Theodore looked at each other.

'Pardon, what did you say?'

'Their newborn baby boy, little Carter.'

'That can't be right, Jara. Grace would have told me that she was . . .'

'I had a brother?' Bea got straight to the point.

'Oh my, oh my, yes, he was a beautiful baby – small, premature by a few weeks, he surprised Gracie and Frankie, and me. I delivered him, you know.'

Theodore was trying to take in the magnitude of events that were unfolding.

'Hang on, you are sure you have the right people? You're not mixing them up with somebody else? They never mentioned anything to us about having a baby.'

Bea spoke up. 'Mummy's letter, she said she had a big surprise. This is a big surprise!'

Theodore and Bunty nodded slowly in time together.

'So you delivered the baby?' Bunty asked Jara, eager to hear more.

'That I did. I'm kind of the midwife around here, delivered a lot of babies, I have; can remember every one like it was my own.'

Theodore, Bunty and Bea were all silent but clearly wanting to know more so Jara continued. 'When they arrived Gracie was already in labour. She was brought straight here.' She folded her arms over her ample body.

'The baby was small but very strong and silent, never cried once. They

stayed here for a few weeks but before they left they were determined to see some Raptors of Paradise and find some temple. I told them there are no temples on these islands and they may only catch a glimpse of a raptor.'

'But why did they take the boy with them?'

'I mean no disrespect, as I know things are different in England, but around here when you have a baby you get up, feed it, swaddle it in a sling and get back to work. I admired Gracie's drive to pick herself up and get on with her life. I showed her how we tie a sling around here and she already knew how to feed the baby. A few days sitting on a kylos while the men chop away at the jungle and make camp is a holiday around here.'

'And why did she leave her clothes here?'

'Everyone thought they were coming back – she did not need them in the jungle, she left the whole case here.'

Bunty and Bea looked at the case and immediately went over to it and delved in.

Bunty picked up an armful of clothes from both Grace and Franklin that were definitely not suitable for the rainforest and went through them all one by one, soaking up their memories.

Bea handed to Theodore quite a few strange artefacts that had probably been gathered along their trip: a small heavy-duty box that was padlocked, a few reading books and a satchel almost identical to hers. Bea paused as she saw Theodore gulp and wipe a small tear from his eye.

'My lord, I gave this to Frank for his birthday to carry his fishing tackle in – looks like it's seen some action!' He poked his finger through a perfect circular hole in one of the front pockets. 'That's a bullet hole, all right! Thankfully this was inside to stop it.' Theodore raised his eyebrows as he pulled out a heavy journal with the offending bullet still deeply imbedded in the centre. Bea had found a sketchbook, almost identical to her own in every way, and she leafed through the many pages of colourful sketches, depictions and notes.

'That was Grace's. Haven't I always told you how similar you are!' Bunty stroked her granddaughter's hair and Bea smiled back with happy tears of joy at finding something so personal of her mother's.

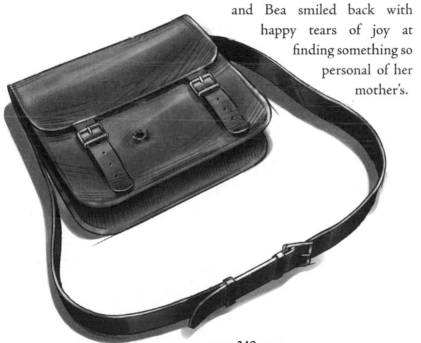

The light in the room momentarily blotted out. Everyone turned and faced the feral boy, who stood in the doorway with the last of the evening light burning behind him, outlining the feathers bound to him with a deep orange glow. In that instant everyone thought the same, very obvious thing, but it was Bea who spoke it aloud.

'I think you are Carter. I know you are.'

It was simply too mind-boggling to comprehend. Bea pulled away from Theodore and stepped over to him, placing a hand on his shoulder.

'That makes you my little brother.'

'Bea, Bunty – how do you know? He doesn't look the right age, he doesn't even look that human!' Theodore tried to be the voice of reason, but his voice was full of anxiety.

'I know it sounds odd and unbelievable, but he's been following me since we came here. I think he knows something is . . . connecting us.'

Bunty stepped forward to them both and knelt down so she could look closer into his eyes.

'Theodore, can't you see Franklin in his eyes?' She went to brush some sand off his cheek and he pulled away quickly, not realising it was a friendly gesture.

'So they're the same blue, but that proves nothing,' Theodore said. 'Biggie has a very good point everyone is overlooking: a baby can't survive in the jungle alone – and why would raptors kill the adults and spare a baby?'

Biggie stepped forward. 'This boy probably comes from another island around here, ran away from home, took refuge here and somehow befriended the raptors, like your friend Kunava.'

Bunty looked puzzled at Theodore.

'But Kunava said you're a Saurman. You said you would look after him.'

'Yes and no. I'm not a Saurman, but I will look after him. We owe this boy our life, after all. I'm just struggling to believe this is Carter Kingsley.'

'We will have time to answer that on the boat, but we have another problem to solve,' Bea said firmly, and everyone turned towards her.

'Biggie, Jara, you will all be in danger when we leave. Hayter will want to know who helped us off the island. You always told me, Theo, that running away is not the answer, fixing the problem is.'

Theodore nodded and Biggie looked to Jara.

'This is true, and you have a plan?'

'No, but I think Sammy does.'

25

The Ginger Prince

~ Great-uncle Bulgaria ~

The morning shift was well underway and the dock was alive with activity as Sammy arrived. The monthly cargo boat was moored at the dock and there was more than the usual chatter amongst the deckhands. There was also a noticeable lack of Hayter's men around to help load the cages onboard and rumour had got out that something was up. Sammy edged his way up the dockside, tethered Junior to a post and whistled, summoning a burst of activity up ahead. Two deckhands jogged down the wooden walkway and Sammy instructed them in the local dialect to help unload the cargo from his new kylos.

'Whose kylos is that, boy?'

Sammy froze in fear at the unmistakeable growl of Christian Hayter, who was sitting in the shade behind the dockhouse.

Sammy decided the best form of defence was attack. 'I've been looking for you.'

'And I've been looking for you. Answer the question – whose kylos is that?'

'I've had to hire him from my Great-uncle Bulgaria over in Dobbo.'

'That so? And where's your other, more colourful one?' Hayter rubbed his chin and spat.

'That is exactly why I have been looking for you.' Sammy squared up to Hayter and also spat on the ground, trying to look just as angry. 'The westerners who came here a week ago said they were your friends. They tricked me and took him. Now I have to use this lump.'

Sammy kicked Junior; the kylos looked back a little puzzled. 'Embarrassing being seen in town with this, bad for business,' Sammy went on. 'You find these filthy friends of yours, get back my Junior without a scratch on his paintwork, and I will forget this happened. I may even pay you a very small reward.'

Sammy looked straight at Hayter and refused to blink. Hayter smiled at the audacity of the boy.

'Okay, lad, you can help me get him.'

'Seriously, don't kid me, I've had a stressful week.'

'I'm short of a kylos and I need your help. I might even pay you, how about it?'

'But I have this load to get rid of,' Sammy said reluctantly. He slapped Junior on the head.

Hayter looked at the two scrawny men struggling to unload the sacks of spice from the kylos's back and went over, taking the largest sack and hurling it to the deck with a thud.

'Careful, you would make a very bad porter.' Sammy told him. 'You will break your back – and the cargo!'

Hayter smirked and slammed the second sack a little harder to the floor. 'Right, follow me.'

Sammy barked a few orders to the deckhands and pointed to the cargo boat before taking the kylos by the chinstrap and following Hayter away from the dock. Eager to look behind, but not wanting to alert Hayter, Sammy pretended that Junior had stood on his toe, yelped and spun around, cursing the saur in several tongues. As he did so he noticed the last two spice sacks that Hayter had unloaded hopping off up the jetty, and smiled. His part of the plan was working, even if he was now diverting off course and following Hayter to find the very kylos he was walking next to.

✦ ✦ ✦

The curtains twitched at the post office, as the postmistress nervously looked out and spied Hayter striding up the street with Sammy following. She let the curtain drop and turned to Bunty, who stood in front of her.

'Tell me again, you want me to do what, exactly?'

'You just have to tell him I came here to send a telegram. He must believe you.'

'That's the problem, lady, he won't believe me. He knows I hate his guts. If I do him a favour he will know something's up.'

'I understand, but we have to all work together or this plan won't work.'

'This is too risky. He will set that terrible Beast on me like he did the last postmaster if he finds out.'

'Look . . .' Bunty tried to find the words that would persuade her. 'Imagine if Hayter and his men left this island. Someone else would have to run it.'

'And who might that be?'

The postmistress crossed her arms and was instantly vexed at the prospect of someone else making all the bad decisions.

'Exactly.' Bunty crossed her arms too.

The postmistress twigged what Bunty was saying and uncrossed her arms as the front door swung open.

'I'm closed!' she shouted out from her office.

'Not for me, you ain't!' Hayter called back and dinked the bell on her counter loudly. Bunty remained in the office and listened to what unfolded as the postmistress burst out of the office and reeled off her usual welcoming torrent of grumpiness.

Suddenly there was the sound of something hard striking the counter and the room fell silent.

Bunty wanted to look but she was frozen in fear.

'You are going to pay for that!'

'So you are open, then?'

'If it means you get out quicker then yes. And get that silly hook weapon off my counter.'

'I have some minor cuts that need ointment, and a bellyache.'

'You look like death, and that's an improvement.'

Hayter blew his cheeks out and raised his eyes to the ceiling to try to find some patience. 'Look, I would love to chat all day but if you don't mind, GET THE MEDICINE CABINET OPEN!'

The postmistress took the keys that hung around her neck and opened the cabinet door with a tut, but not before a quick look into the mirror to remove her postmistress hat and replace it with a nurse's bonnet.

'Surgical spirit is the strongest I have, should clean the wounds, and this, it's just bicarbonate of soda but if you put a spoonful in some whiskey it will taste better and fix you up.'

Hayter grabbed them out of her hands. 'Put it on my tab.'

'That and a new desk!' she retorted and continued under her breath, 'Now get out, you loathsome little rat.'

The door slammed shut and the whole building shook. Bunty peered around the corner.

'You didn't tell him about the telegram! I thought you were going to help?'

The postmistress let herself cool down for a moment before stepping back into the office.

'Like I said, it's not in my nature to be helpful, especially to a man like that, and he would be suspicious of me if I tried to be. But I have a plan. My ever-so-useless son could prove to have some usefulness after all.'

The postmistress gave a long comical wink to Bunty and swung around to the telegram machine. 'What do you want the telegram to say?'

Bunty dictated a short note to an old friend that they had come into a spot of bother in the Islands of Aru and planned to slip unnoticed off the island from the Old Town. To make it more believable, she also requested a new change of clothes as some horrid man had burned them all.

'Good. Now for the final part of the puzzle. SHUGGY, come here now, boy!'

Shuggy stepped into the room and shrugged. 'What?'

'I'll what you in a minute with a big stick. Come here, I have a job for you.'

Bunty saw something that might help sweeten the situation and took down a glass jar from the highest shelf of the office.

'Excuse me, Shuggy,' Bunty said, then paused as the postmistress and Shuggy looked up at her. 'I was wondering if you would do something for all of us, and if you do, I will buy you this whole jar of candied ginger.'

Shuggy's eyes lit up.

The postmistress winked at Bunty and handed the telegram to her son. 'Now, my boy, give this to that rat outside, but don't just give it to him, ask for money first, you understand?'

Shuggy looked back at Bunty with the ginger and held out his hand.

'First you give me the ginger, lady.'

The postmistress ruffled his hair proudly. 'That's my ginger prince, you know how to bargain.'

+ + +

Hayter ran out from the bar and spat a white foaming substance onto the ground and wiped his frothing mouth on his sleeve. He ran his tongue over his teeth and spat again before uncorking the bottle of surgical spirit he was carrying and pouring some on his dirty handkerchief. He peeled the damp shirt from his body and slapped the alcohol-soaked handkerchief directly onto his skin where the majority of the arrow wounds were. The pain was instant and the discomfort great; he was in public, with what could be a tear soon to be rolling down his cheek. Hayter turned away, but to his horror Shuggy was standing there, looking straight up at him, holding out a telegram, asking for money and smelling of ginger.

26

A Chorus of Distress

~ no plan B ~

Biggie had drunk too much coffee that morning and it was the third time he had mentioned to Theodore that he needed to have a pee.

'Just hang on and wait here, old boy.' Theodore tried to calm Biggie's nerves. 'If everyone does their bit we should be able to get into the depot in no time at all.'

'That's what I'm worried about – what if the plan falls apart and we have to sit here for hours?'

'It will work, trust me.'

Biggie had been tipped off early that morning that all the hunters had been found screaming in pain sooner than hoped for, and some had already returned to New Town with some help. The *Orca* was not due to come back for another day so the group would need to change their escape vessel. They now needed a distraction so they could all get smuggled aboard the cargo boat instead. Sammy's plan had been hatched over breakfast with not much time to think it through; there was no plan B.

Biggie and Theodore had hidden in some bushes close

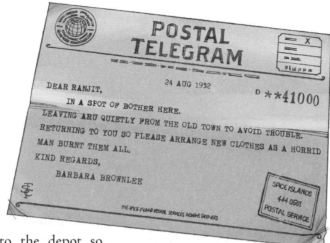

POSTAL
TELEGRAM

DEAR RANJIT,
    IN A SPOT OF BOTHER HERE.
LEAVING ARU QUIETLY FROM THE OLD TOWN TO AVOID TROUBLE.
RETURNING TO YOU SO PLEASE ARRANGE NEW CLOTHES AS A HORRID
MAN BURNT THEM ALL.
KIND REGARDS,
    BARBARA BROWNLEE

24 AUG 1932

D ✳✳41000

SPICE ISLANDS
444 0581
POSTAL SERVICE

to the depot so
they could see the comings and goings
close up without being noticed. Biggie nudged Theodore
again and pointed. Hayter was pacing up the road but
he was not alone; they could see Sammy following with
Junior.

'There's Sammy! Why is he here? This was not in the
plan!'

Biggie was obviously spiralling into a panic so
Theodore tried to calm him.

'I'm not sure what has happened, Biggie, but your boy
is the bravest young man I know. He's up to something, so
let's trust him.'

Hayter whistled loudly and all his men dropped what
they were doing and gathered around. He presented
what looked like a telegram to them, waved it about, then

ripped it into tiny pieces and threw the pieces in the air so the paper snowed down onto them all. With that, the men scurried off and started to ready themselves to leave.

'Okay, so it looks like Hayter's taken the bait as we originally planned, but what's he doing with Sammy?' Theodore pondered as he looked about the yard. It was void of any saurs: the pen that usually held the kylos was empty except for an old donkey.

'Okay, there's good news and there's bad news.'

'I only like good news,' Biggie said.

'Well, the good news is that yesterday in the jungle we freed all of Hayter's kylos and mimus. So the bad news is he now only has a donkey to carry all their equipment, so he needs Sammy to help out.'

'To trap you in the Old Town?'

'Looks like it.'

'Well, that's all right for you, because you're not going to be in the Old Town, you're going to be on a boat far from here.'

Theodore looked guiltily at Biggie, remembering Bea being so clear that running away caused bigger problems for everyone that was left behind.

'Sammy's master plan, if followed through perfectly, gets us all off the island, yes. And our part is to distract Hayter enough so that whilst we slip away on the cargo boat you have time to pack up your family and move away from here to somewhere safer,' Theodore said.

Biggie bit his lip and thought deeply.

'Yes, but running away does not solve all the problems.' He sighed deeply as he concluded, 'The big problem is how to get Hayter and his men off the island for ever, so the island doesn't have to be ravaged by them any more. They are the ones who should leave, not us.'

It was a terrible fifteen minutes waiting for Hayter and his men to gather everything and watch Sammy at work loading Junior. As the procession hurried past the bushes in the direction of the dock Biggie closed his eyes and Theodore held his shoulder in support. When everyone was safely out of sight, Theodore leant in and said, 'I'm sure this will work out. Now, let's get to work – and you can have that pee now.'

✦ ✦ ✦

'Carter, stop it!'

Bea knew the boy couldn't understand the words but hoped that he might realise what she was trying to get him to do, which was to stay still. It was their turn to be piled onto a sack trolley and rolled up the jetty to the cargo boat, and the boy had wiggled around to peek through some convenient air-holes in the sacking. He was used to being in a sack; he had after all slept in one for most of his life. Bea, however, was starting to get itchy and anxious, even though she had heard Sammy coolly talking his way out of danger when Hayter had accosted him on the dock.

The men on the boat were not alarmed by wriggling sacks. Transporting livestock of all shapes and sizes was an art and the boat was kitted out with gullies under the cages so excrement could be hosed down and washed away at sea. This did nothing for the stench that hummed and seeped through the sack fabric. Thankfully Bea and the boy were tipped out on an upper deck where the air was sweeter, straight onto a larger pile of sacks containing spices and other dry goods. When it became quiet, Bea manoeuvred herself so that she too could spy out of an air-hole in the sack. The coast was clear . . . but the boy was already half out of his bag.

'Carter, wait!'

It was no use, the boy was out as quick as a flash, and searching for Bea's sack by prodding each one in turn. Bea was still struggling to get out when the boy slashed

her sack open with one of his raptor claws in a move that almost took out her eye. She started to tell him off but he held his hand over her mouth and rolled them both under the sack pile as another two heavy bags landed close to where they had just been. Lying on top of her yet again, his face filled her view; his quick reflexes had saved her once more.

When it quietened down, Carter leapt up, pulled Bea over to a dark corner and then crouched down. Bea started to talk again but he quickly held one finger up and tapped his ear twice. The boy was working out a plan now, but sadly it was not the one hatched by Sammy, which had Bea and Carter remaining in their sacks until they felt the boat's engines start. After a while on the open sea Theodore would get out of his sack first and find Bunty, Bea and Carter, reuniting them all. But the boy had his own plan.

Carter's eyes darted about as some of the livestock below decks started a chorus of distress. His eyes flared and he rustled his arm feathers. Bea could see he was intently listening to the myriad noises, trying to pick out certain ones. Suddenly he shrieked.

'*Quarrk, quarrk?*'

Bea shook her head. 'Shhhh, be quiet!'

'*Quarrk quarrk?*' he called out again and, from a distant corner of the boat came a reply:

'*Quarrk, quarrk!*'

The boy turned to Bea and pushed her further into the corner, preparing to leave. She whispered at him to stop, but he pushed her again, harder. Bea grabbed his arm and gave him a look of defiance Bunty herself would have been proud of. Something obviously got through this time as he shrugged and took her hand, leading her towards an open hatch to the level below.

27

Friends in High Places

~ this gesture of freedom ~

'Well done, Bunty old girl.' Theodore smiled as he checked that the depot was as empty as it looked. The telegram diversion had done its trick. Turning to Biggie, he said, 'The depot is bigger than I remember, have we got enough explosive?'

Biggie smiled for the first time that day. 'Now it's your turn to trust me. We do and now is the time to use it. This place is usually full of caged creatures for export. The only time it's empty is when the cargo boat takes them all away. This is our only chance to destroy the building and not harm a fly.'

'So where do you want me?' Theodore clapped his hands together, impatient to start.

'It will just take a stick on each of the supports and the whole building will come down. Let me handle the TNT and you tie them in place with this.' He threw Theodore a roll of fuse wire. 'Then we need some in the supply hut after I have liberated some items, and finally the rest goes on the refrigeration plant.'

'I thought the plant wasn't working, so why do we need to bother?'

'It does work. I just removed a fuse. Soon Hayter will find out it's not the spare part that he has been waiting on that will fix the problem.'

Theodore nodded. 'Good trick, Biggie. That will have saved thousands of small lives.' He paused, thinking. 'So how long will it take for Hayter to rebuild his empire?'

'Well, he will be angry, ruthless and out setting traps the very next day, I expect, but he won't have a depot to store his catches or a refrigeration plant to freeze them for about six months.'

'Six months. Better than nothing, but it's not that long.'

'Hayter has friends in high places – that man did not get this job based on his cleverness. Makes me think he's placed here to do other people's dirty work and he is too dumb to realise it,' Biggie said.

They linked the last pillar and moved on to the next task as Theodore mulled it all over in his head.

'Was Hayter in charge when Franklin and Grace came here?'

'Things were better back then, we had a Dutchman in charge. There was a good trade in spices and just a small amount of feathers were traded with the indigenous people here, men like Kunava – the man I knew, not your claw-handed tribesman.' Biggie winked at Theodore and mimed attacking him with two claws. 'Then someone bought the trading rights to this island and Hayter came soon after. Put him in charge of taking everything with a value from the island. The Dutchman put up a brave fight but he was useless against Hayter and his Black Tyrant.'

◆ ◆ ◆

Bea had followed Carter down the wide steps, and when she came to the last rung her feet were submerged in an ankle-deep puddle of dark liquid. She shuddered to think what it was made from; it was definitely contributing to the acrid smell. This smell was probably what kept the deckhands upstairs. Their shadows slid past the narrow gaps in the floorboards above and broke up the razor-sharp beams of light that shone down onto everything below.

The boy came to the first stack of cages that contained some of the shadow raptors captured in the deadly raid under the rainbow tree. The hull was packed several cages high with frantic animals and birds either trying to escape or slumped, motionless piles of fur and feathers, too weak to fight any more. The sight was heartbreaking.

'Carter, what are you doing?' Bea whispered.

Carter was trying to work the intricate lock on the cages whilst communicating to the shadow raptors with a rhythmical *whoot-whoot* calming sound. He turned and *whooted* at Bea, whilst slapping the lock a few times.

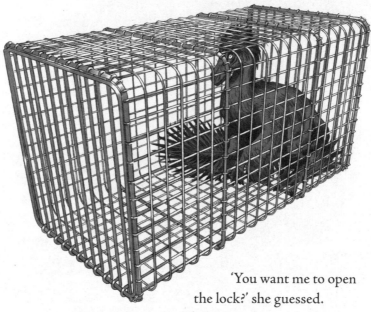

'You want me to open the lock?' she guessed.

She pointed to it and got a more excited *whoot-whoot* in return.

'No, no, no – we can't get them out.' She tried to reason with the boy and show it by shaking both her hands. 'We can't let them free, we will be discovered here – they will kill us all!'

The boy slapped the cage harder and *whooted* more persistently, but Bea was starting to get flustered.

'The plan is when we are at sea, away from danger, we persuade the ship's captain to land on another island and free everything there. Bunty said she would happily pay the captain to do so.'

She held her hands up higher and continued to shake them with what she thought was the internationally recognised gesture for 'stop this now'. That set of rules did not apply to the animal kingdom, however, and the boy ignored her, continuing to tackle the lock until suddenly the cage door swung open. Bea was knocked back as the raptor jumped out and stumbled but managed to stop herself from falling into the dark liquid that sloshed about on the floor. Carter, having now worked out how to open the tricky locks, started on the second cage.

'Carter, stop it now, please!'

But it was too late. Before she knew what was happening, the quickly put-together plan was spiralling out of control. There was no way Bea would be able to get the raptors back into the cages. She stood back and let Carter open up more locks. The boy was blissfully unaware that this gesture of freedom would be what sealed their own untimely end, Bea thought. There was nothing more to do except help him . . .

✦ ✦ ✦

Christian Hayter stopped by the side of the path, waved Sammy and his men past, then held out a hand when Ash and Bishop walked by and pulled them to one side.

'Lads, something is not right. Ash, you follow your nose, go ahead with the men and stake out the Old Town. Stay in the treeline and keep an eye on our friends.'

'Gotcha, boss.'

'Keep them there and don't do anything heroic until I get back with Bishop. We're heading back to bring out the Beast.'

Bishop gulped. 'I think the Beast is sleeping, boss,' he said, but Hayter gave him a cold look in return.

'Well, I guess you'll just have to go wake him up now, won't you?'

◆ ◆ ◆

Theodore looked at his watch. 'How much longer, Biggie?'

'You head off now, my friend, get down to the dock and find Bunty. I will have to stay and manually charge the fuse wire as I have no timers.'

'Hang on, you said –'

'I lied. Besides I hate saying goodbyes.'

Theodore was well aware that this was it. But he was reluctant to go.

'Biggie, promise me you will get your family away from this doomed island.'

'Blast!' Biggie interrupted Theodore and pulled him behind the store shed. 'Hayter's coming back, look!'

'Great Scott, why is he back so soon?'

Biggie forced his hand into Theodore's and quickly gave it a good shake. 'You need to get out of here fast, you hear – fast!'

Theodore nodded. 'Farewell my friend, until the next time.'

Biggie smiled. 'Please don't come here again. I mean that with the fondest wishes.'

Theodore smiled back and, as Hayter and Bishop turned into the yard behind the depot, darted off down the dirt road towards the dock.

28

Saddling the Beast

~ joyful shrieks of freedom ~

Biggie crept along the treeline around the back of the hut to try to discover why Hayter had returned. As soon as he did, it became chillingly apparent. The Dwarf Black Tyrant Hayter called 'the Beast' was chained up under a tree, asleep. The dry earth around it was covered in deep grooves where the tyrant had tried to burrow out; nearby there was a wooden post that had a shorter chain attached to it. On further inspection it appeared to have been reinforced; it looked like something was often chained to it and served as dinner. A high wooden fence obscured the view from the back of the depot so the tyrant could not usually be seen.

Biggie watched as Hayter and his right-hand man quietly loosened the end of the chain from the tree. It was in fact two chains, and the Beast was harnessed to them by a metal collar around its neck. Hayter and Bishop tiptoed in opposite directions carrying a chain each and re-tethered the ends to metal stakes a little further away, limiting its movement to just a few inches. As they did so it awoke and tried to stand, but was restrained from doing so by the newly repositioned chains. 'Now then, my lovely boy, you be good and let us put this saddle on you. Then I will take you for a stroll to get some lunch . . . fresh human food,' crooned Hayter.

The tyrant pulled and twisted violently at its chains for a good few minutes before it stopped resisting. Meanwhile Bishop came out of the store shed with a large saddle.

'Right, Bishop, you know what to do.'

Bishop nodded nervously as he crept up from behind, keeping away from the tyrant's tail.

'That's it, he can't see you from there.'

If the chain had not been shortened, saddling the Beast would have been impossible. Biggie had seen the Dwarf Black Tyrant on a few occasions but no one had ever seen where it was kept or how Hayter had managed to tame it. Fitting one with a specially widened allosaur saddle was one thing, riding it was a whole other level. Biggie had seen images from exotic places around the world of people riding tyrants – even as a boy he remembered a wooden toy with a Roman Emperor riding a White Titan Tyrant that his father had given him. But Dwarf Blacks like this were a very rare sight, known to be found only on Flores, further up the island chains that made up Indonesia. This tyrant was just like all the other creatures that came into contact with Christian Hayter. Sad, beaten, tormented and taken from its natural home, this creature was just bigger and more dangerous than the rest.

The tyrant's slick black-feathered body shone in the heat of the day with an oily shimmer of reflective green and blue highlights. Its densely packed muscular form rippled as it continued to resist the saddle and when Bishop swung the bridle around its head it opened its huge jaw wide, allowing him to secure the bit at the back of its mouth and revealing all its serrated teeth as it clenched down on the metal. The more Bishop strapped it in, the more it fought, until Hayter unclipped his bullhook and raised it in front of its face.

'You want to be a good boy for Daddy now, or you'll taste the end of this.'

The tyrant's resistance faded away as it recognised the pain the hook could inflict.

Biggie crept back along the trees and snuck into the store shed, grabbed his kit bag and finished setting the last stick that had been daisy-chained to all the others around the depot. Tossing the fuse wire out of the window, he darted outside and

ran it out as far as he could towards the trees. He dropped to the ground and set about the fiddly task of wiring up the detonator.

Then came a roar so chilling Biggie knew his time was running out. Hayter was now parading around behind the depot riding the Beast. Biggie stripped the last wire with his teeth and frantically wound it around the last contact point. Looking up, he raised the charger arm and waited. Thirty seconds later Hayter trotted into view from the side of the depot, right next to the store shed, the perfect position. Biggie plunged the charger arm down and closed his eyes tight, counting down, bracing for the blast.

'Eight, nine, ten . . . eleven? Twelve?'

Nothing happened.

Biggie opened his eyes. Hayter was still there astride the Beast. Bishop was trying to untangle something that was caught on the end of the tyrant's tail. So Biggie recharged the detonator and plunged the arm down for a second time.

And then a third.

Something was not working – he desperately looked at the detonator's connection points and then followed the wire with his eye along the floor all the way to where it stopped . . . in Bishop's hand. The Beast's legs had got caught in the fuse wire.

He could hear Hayter barking at Bishop. 'It's fuse wire, you idiot, this place has been booby-trapped!'

He turned and the Beast stood high and roared almightily again, the sound reverberating around the town.

'You stay here and un-wire this. I'm off to the dock. We've been set up!'

+ + +

'What's going on down there?'

A thick shaft of sunlight beamed down from the open hatch. Bea had been waiting on the other side for this moment. Here was there only chance to get off the doomed boat and to try to find Theodore and Bunty.

'Help! I've been trapped down here with all these wild creatures!'

Her acting was borderline truthful and her presence was enough to puzzle the deckhand, who held out a hand and helped her up, only to be thanked by Bea clocking him over the head with a plank of wood, knocking him out cold. She quickly jumped out of the way as Carter led the charge, with all the other raptors, birds and animals following closely behind.

Bea watched as they poured out from below deck in a constant mass until every last creature had made its way up and out. The original plan may have failed but she knew that releasing the creatures was the correct thing to do. She picked up one of the last Short-tailed Raptors of Paradise that was hopping on a broken foot and followed the exodus off the cargo boat and down the jetty to the dock. The sky was thick with exotic birds and

the air filled with their joyful shrieks of freedom.

Bea stopped at the end of the jetty. She was halfway around the world from her home and wondering what way to turn.

'Beatrice, what's happening?'

Bea turned. Where Hayter had been sitting earlier that day in the shade of the dockhouse was a stack of wooden barrels. Bea spun all around looking for the familiar voice.

'Beatrice! I'm over here!'

She looked back as the lid of one of the barrels tilted and out popped her grandmother's head.

'Quick, jump in and hide. The one next to me is empty!'

29

Barrel Smashing

~ *this is a good game* ~

The Beast could not decide which way to turn. Hayter was trying to get it to head straight for the dock but a torrent of birds and animals were streaming past within tempting biting distance. Hayter could see all his last month's hard work running away. He urged the Beast furiously towards the dock, where the torrent was now just a trickle of the slowest-moving creatures that could not keep up with the others.

The tyrant slowed down and sniffed the ground.

'What you found, boy?'

Hayter manoeuvred the Beast as it followed its nose up to a barrel over by the dockhouse.

A Lesser Bird of Paradise was slumped up against it, unable to move, and it let out a defiant cry as the Dwarf Black Tyrant plucked it up with its jaws, tossed it high into the air then snapped it down whole in one bite.

Hayter turned the Beast quickly to face up the street, trying to spot Logan and his friends, but as he did so the tyrant whipped its tail and smashed it into the side of the

dockhouse, spilling all the barrels over the floor. The lid rolled off one and out fell Bunty. The Beast's glowing yellow eyes saw her before Hayter did: it immediately lunged at her, snagging her skirt in its front teeth, dragging her up, then dropping her so it could go in for a better bite.

'Hold it, boy, HOLD IT!'

Hayter pulled on the reins and the Beast stopped inches away from Bunty, who was cowering below it. The tyrant breathed in deeply and then roared ferociously in her face, sending saliva all over her and causing her to faint. She flopped back unconscious to the ground.

'Good boy. Hold it and wait for my command . . .'

He stroked its neck but before Hayter could issue the order to kill, Theodore jumped in with a plank of wood and swung at the Beast's head.

'Take –' and smashing the plank in two – 'that!'

The tyrant barely registered the blow. With one swift sideways swipe of its head, Theodore was flying through the air, landing ten yards away. He stumbled to his feet only to be swiped off them again, this time by the Beast's sleek black tail.

Hayter could not contain his joy and laughed out loud.

Bunty started coming round; slowly she inched herself out of the way.

'Where is that wretched saur boy and that horrid girl?'

Bunty and Theodore were silent.

'Let's see if they're hiding in the barrels.' Hayter pulled on the reins and sent the tyrant around to sniff at a barrel, before stamping on it, breaking it into pieces.

'Stop it!' Bunty cried out.

'No, this is a good game. One down, three to go!'

The Beast lunged in for the second barrel and stamped it into splinters.

'Two missing animals and two barrels left. Perfect odds. Let's choose one.'

Bunty froze and Hayter mimed eeny-meeny-miny-moe, pointing back and forth to the two remaining barrels.

'Bea, get out now!' screamed Bunty.

But it was too late. Hayter's finger landed on the nearest barrel and the tyrant placed its large foot on it and toyed with it before slamming down hard.

Hayter looked down eagerly but there was nothing but shattered wood.

'Well, you cried out to Bea, so I'm guessing the last one must contain the little rat. Beast, she is all yours!'

The tyrant spun the final barrel around so it could get a better purchase, before opening its jaws wide and picking it up from one end. It lifted it high in one fluid movement, whipping its muscular neck upwards before letting go and eagerly watching it fly through the air and smash to the floor. With its tongue hanging out, it paced over to the shattered barrel, expecting to finally have its kill, only to be gravely disappointed by yet more wood splinters.

'You looking for me?'

Bea stepped out from what was left of the dockhouse with a loose coil of rope in her hands. Theodore had managed to drag himself over to Bunty and motioned frantically for her to get back, but it was too late. It had taken a while for Hayter to get the Beast to stop sniffing at the broken barrel, but now it turned. Hayter glared down at her.

'No darts to help you this time.'

'No darts, but I have this.'

And with that she yanked at the coiled rope. It slid out from under the broken door, a grappling hook with

a slightly putrid fish gouged onto one of the three spikes.

She tugged it again and the Beast locked its gaze to the fish. Not only did it look interesting but it smelt interesting. Bea tugged it a third time and its eyes followed the rope.

'And what are you going to do with that?' Hayter smirked.

Bea glared back up at him.

'Your Dwarf Black Tyrant is just a bit bigger and more stupid than my thoroughbred allosaur, and even Rusty, with his bigger brain, loves to play this.'

Bunty and Theodore nodded at each other. They knew instantly the game she meant.

Bea gave a high-pitched whistle and tugged at the rope so that the fish twitched again. The tyrant stared at it and a long drool of saliva dripped from the corner of its mouth. Bea knew she had its full attention. With that she ran off, dragging the grappling hook behind her so that the fish twitched and flipped as it hit every bump and stone. The Beast could not resist and bolted after it, jerking Hayter about in the saddle. Its head low, it tried to snap at the fish as Bea moved it left then right, darting back and forth as she ran, always one step ahead.

'Whoa! Hold it! HOLD IT! Beast, STOP!' Hayter dragged on the reins. But it was no good. The tyrant turned and twisted, trying to get the fish on the hook.

Then Bea doubled back on herself, but unknowingly

left too much slack. As she ran, the grappling hook remained motionless long enough for the Beast to swipe the fish from it in one clean move. Then it turned its attention to Bea.

The Dwarf Black Tyrant turned and lunged at her, ripping the straps of her dress and catching the collar of her mother's frilled blouse in its massive teeth. It lifted her her right up. Fortunately the blouse was a good few sizes too big: Bea slid right out of the bottom and dropped to the floor. Not realising that Bea was no longer inside, the Beast continued to shred her clothing. Hayter had realised, however, and dug his heels in hard and yanked the reins. As soon as the tyrant saw Bea it lunged again and missed as she ducked and attempted to run over to where Theodore and Bunty lay wounded. The tyrant took another two paces with its big strides, caught up, kicked Bea over and clamped its huge padded foot on top of her, its sharp talons pinning Bea to the floor like a cat tormenting a wounded mouse. She tried to scrabble out.

'Stay still and play dead!' Theodore cried out.

It was too late. The tyrant dipped its mighty head down for the fatal bite . . . but Hayter pulled hard on the reins. 'Where's the saur boy? Tell me . . . or the girl is lunch.'

Bunty and Theodore were all out of ideas. Suddenly the tyrant whipped its head round to face a large clan of shadow raptors that had converged behind them. In the centre defiantly stood the boy, the fresh application of crushed red achiote fruit to his face making his cold blue eyes stand out like sapphires in blood. The raptors had flushed their faces an angry red and stared intently at the enormous tyrant before them. Bea could see just how well her long-lost younger brother had assimilated himself with his surrogate family.

Hayter laughed out loud.

'Is this a challenge, boy? You're no match for a tyrant.'

The Beast opened its jaws wide and screeched a long and chilling roar that shook the raptors' feathers. Still the boy stood defiant and motionless and stared straight at the tyrant. As it roared, something that the boy recognised had caught the light and sparkled in the back of its mouth. He glanced down at Bea and then narrowed his eyes at the tyrant who had just finished issuing its almighty threat.

The raptors and the boy lunged their heads forward with a hiss and fanned out their long neck feathers in a startling display. The Dwarf Black Tyrant sized up the fight ahead by swinging its head from left to right and rattled its massive jaw. Somehow this created a haunting shivering sound that spooked both raptor and human alike – all except Hayter, astride the Beast, who just laughed. The boy let out a short hiss in return and, alone, stepped a few paces forward, keeping direct eye contact with the tyrant, who slowly turned its head to follow him. Hayter tugged the reins again to swing the Beast around. The tyrant finally had to release Bea to keep its balance on its two powerful feet. Bea crawled back over to Theodore and Bunty who dragged her close and held onto her.

'Boy, this is pointless. You seriously want to take on my Beast alone?' He laughed at the odds stacked against his victim.

Carter continued to circle the tyrant.

30

The Bullhook

~ a nasty, pointless death ~

With his eyes fixed on the tyrant, the boy slowly pulsated his arms in and out, in and out, so that his long display feathers flapped to the rhythm of his heartbeat. With each pulse the feathers lifted a little further, until eventually they became fully extended. Then he started to arch and lower his head, bending his knees with every beat of his wings.

'What's Carter doing?' Bea whispered to Theodore who was holding her close.

'I don't know.'

The Beast had started to inhale and exhale with every flap of Carter's wings. The tyrant had almost completely lowered itself to the ground and was now crouching on the floor, pivoting in a circle. The boy was now nearly within touching distance of the huge saur, so low to the ground his wide wing flaps were sending up dust clouds.

He could feel the tyrant's hot breath being released in time with his own.

The boy's wings gradually slowed so that the pulsating was now a gentle flap. The tyrant was staring so intently at the boy's eyes it was not aware that his wings had slowed, then finally stopped. Its head was now level with the ground and the boy's wings were pointing directly towards its muzzle. Everyone was spellbound: atop the tyrant, even Hayter's curiosity compelled him to wait and find out what was happening. Bea watched closely. Without a glimmer of fear her new brother was crouching down, arms outstretched, within biting distance of the sleek Black Dwarf Tyrant.

The boy stepped back one pace as far as his legs would take him and dragged his finger along the ground, away from the tyrant's face. The Beast was now flat on its belly, completely transfixed. In a deep state of hypnosis, it stared blankly at the line that had been drawn in the dirt.

The boy turned his head to look over at Bea, Bunty and Theodore with a wide grin on his face. Bea gave him the thumbs up and he returned the unfamiliar gesture.

He then walked straight up to the mesmerised beast, gently patted it on the nose, then lightly ran his hands down to its cheeks and hugged its face. He laid his head to one side and rested it on the tyrant's brow. Both breathed so perfectly in time together that, with each inhalation, the boy was lifted several inches higher. Pulling away, he knelt before the Beast. With both hands he held onto its top and bottom jaw and, with some effort, pulled it open as wide as it would go.

Hayter, mesmerised himself, suddenly snapped out of it and realised what was going on. He dug in his heels but instead of finding the Beast's usual tightly coiled muscles and solid mass its flesh was relaxed and unmoving.

'Get him, you idiot!' he screamed and kicked but there was no reaction from the huge tyrant. It was in its own little world, happily staring at the line on the ground before it.

The boy ignored Hayter and stared deeply into the tyrant's gaping mouth, inspecting its razor-sharp teeth. He gently poked his hand in and felt the tip of one, marvelling at it. A splinter of wooden barrel was lodged into its gum and looked to be painful, so he gently plucked it out and tossed it away. The boy then placed his head directly into the massive saur's open mouth, looked at the back rows and found what he was looking for. With his free hand he reached in and retrieved Bea's necklace and locket, which were looped around a huge back tooth. Wiping the spittle and last remaining parts of its dinner from the locket he held it in his hands and carefully examined the two black-and-white heads within. Snapping it shut, he stepped back then patted the Beast on the nose. It remained motionless with its mouth hanging wide open, saliva forming long gloopy drips. With both hands he pushed on the tyrant's jaws and gently closed its mouth. Above, Hayter was screaming and kicking but nothing was getting through to the mighty saur.

The boy walked over to Bea and handed the necklace to her.

Bea was almost speechless. 'Thank you, Carter.'

Like the tyrant, Bunty and Theodore had their mouths hanging open in disbelief.

'Carter?' the boy replied. Bea smiled and threw her arms around him, squeezed tight and gave her first ever hug to her new brother.

'Get up, you stupid saur!' Hayter's commands to the tyrant went unheard.

Unwrapping himself from Bea, Carter walked back to the Beast, fixing his gaze now on Christian Hayter, who

was frantically kicking it. Placing one foot on the tyrant's bottom lip and grabbing its cheekbones the boy placed his other foot on top of its muzzle and confidently walked up the Beast's head as if it was nothing more than climbing over a fallen tree across a ditch.

Dipping both his skinny hands into his waistband, he pulled out and held high his two sharpened shadow raptor claws. He hissed at Hayter, who pulled himself back in the saddle. Stunned at the boy's bravery he unclipped his bullhook and raised it high.

'Stop this! He's just a boy!' Bea called out. 'What do you want with him, what's he done to you?'

'He's an animal, not a boy!' screamed Hayter and with that he swiped down low and hard, not at Carter but into the tyrant's neck, digging the metal claw into the Beast's flesh. The Beast roared out in pain, its trance brutally shattered. It reared up and rattled out another deep blood-curdling roar, forcing Carter to step back and flip backwards off the tyrant's head to the ground.

Hayter grinned. The boy's little hypnotising trick was over and he was back in control.

The Beast swung round and whipped its tail forward, forcing Carter to leap over it; the return swipe was aimed high but he saw it coming and rolled under and away from it. Springing to his feet he darted between the tyrant's legs, forcing Hayter to spin the Beast again to try to keep the boy in view. But Carter knew where its blind spots were

and leapt up onto its foot, wrapping his arm around its calf, holding on tight. Hayter tried to work out where he had gone and saw the boy's arm down at the tyrant's side. Out of frustration he swiped again with his bullhook.

'Shake him off, you idiot!'

But as he looked back the saur boy had swung himself further under and out of sight.

'Where are you now, you little saur boy?'

Hayter was frantically digging in his heels, pulling on the reins in all directions and laying again and again into the side of the Beast's neck with the bullhook, each time puncturing the skin and hitting nerves in the tyrant's neck that were electrifying and painful. The Beast staggered and tried to shake both humans off, whipping its tail about, making the shadow raptors flap desperately backwards out of its way. It was too much for Carter to maintain his hidden position under the saur's belly and he slipped off just as the tyrant started to buck. The huge saur lifted high off the ground and then slammed back down. Hayter jolted forward, dropped the reins and almost slipped but he swiped his weapon, hooked it into the tyrant's neck and kept it there.

The Beast let out another tormented roar of pure pain.

Hayter regained his poise and spotted Carter, who stood flanked by his clan of shadow raptors. 'Kill him, kill all of them, Beast!'

Hayter twisted the bullhook, sending an agonised shiver right through the tyrant.

Carter stood his ground and chirped a command. The clan flared their crimson halo of hidden head feathers and hissed.

'Charge them!'

Hayter twisted the handle of the hook to ratchet up the pain but it was the last straw for the tyrant. It buckled in agony, its right leg crumpling as the nerves sent lightning down it. The saur stumbled and slammed hard into the ground, sending out a shockwave of dust and debris. Carter screeched and the shadow raptors launched themselves at the fallen tyrant. The boy ran over and helped them drag a screaming Hayter from the saddle.

Bunty closed her eyes and turned away.

'You can look, Grandma, they're not killing him.'

Bunty opened one eye cautiously, and then both – Boa was right. The raptors were pinning Hayter to the floor and intimidating him by nipping his skin, but only just scratching at the surface. His screams for mercy were drowned out by their enraged hisses. Carter leapt to the aid of the tyrant, which was twitching in shock and hyperventilating. He smoothed his hands over its muzzle and *whoop-whooped* a calming rhythmic chant to it. Gently lifting the bullhook handle, he slowly withdrew the metal from where it was embedded in the tyrant's neck. Its unusually dark red blood looked more like squid ink as it flowed through the slickly intertwined black feathers. The Beast let out a long breath of relief; it seemed to deflate into the ground where it lay. Carter held on and looked deeply into its eye that lost its focus and blackened before him.

Bea stood up. 'Is it all right?' She ran over to Carter, who looked up with tear-filled eyes as the last of the tyrant's breath rattled out of its mouth.

Bunty looked over to where Carter was stroking its large face. 'Oh, the poor creature. It does not look good at all! Theodore, what can we do?'

Theodore came over and scanned the tyrant with a practised eye. 'There is something we can do, quick everyone, help me get the saddle off it!'

With that he whipped out his knife and cut away the straps that bound the saddle, releasing the tyrant from its tightly twisted bondage. Bunty and Bea pulled the saddle off and suddenly the wounded saur's lungs inflated. Carter squealed with joy as life flooded back into the dazed Beast.

Bea looked round at Theodore, who slipped his knife back into its sheath.

'Theo, that was quick thinking – how did you know?'

'I learnt that the hard way, in the war. We lost a lot of good allosaurs when they fell. The saddle rigging can cut off their air supply. It's a nasty pointless death.'

31

The Hero's Return

~ a unanimous vote ~

The townsfolk had gathered around Hayter and the Beast. The spectacle had been witnessed by everyone and they now wanted to get a closer look at the man and the saur they had feared for so long.

'Get them off me! Help, I'll do anything you want – just get them off me!'

Hayter's pathetic cries echoed out but no one offered any help as the raptors continued to menace him.

Bea knelt close and helped Carter bring some comfort to the exhausted tyrant. She was a little puzzled when he called to a shadow raptor and it started licking the wounds clean, but the raptor's attention certainly did the trick. Theodore also took an interest in this. He rotated his shoulder and arm, then ran his fingers over the bullet wound that was healing unusually fast and without pain. His final arm swing went wide and just missed Bunty.

'That was a good hiding place, Bunty – I was looking all over for you!'

'Well, you obviously did not try hard enough, did you?' She nudged him in the side. 'What do you think of the boy now?'

'There has been only one man I have ever known to command a tyrant like that, and that was Franklin.' Theodore looked down at her. 'We may never find out the whole truth about Grace and Franklin, but I'm sure as sure that that's their boy Carter.'

Bunty nodded her head with a smile in agreement.

The postmistress pulled herself away from the jeering crowd and walked up to them both. 'And how does this solve things, eh? What are we to do when his men return?'

Theodore waved at Bea to come over with Carter.

'She's right. And we still have another situation that needs our attention – Sammy. He's in trouble.'

Bea gasped. 'What trouble?'

'He is in the Old Town with Hayter's men. We need to help him.'

Hayter was trying to get up but had a clan of shadow raptors sitting on him.

'I know what to do,' Bea said.

Theodore looked at her and raised an eyebrow. 'Do what?'

'I'll need your gun.' She held out her hand.

'Beatrice, no!' Bunty was as shocked as the postmistress at her request, but then something else took her attention. 'Hang on a minute – you let that dreadful man get the better of us all and you had your gun with you the whole time?'

Theodore stroked his moustache and thought deeply before speaking. 'Sure I did. A gun is the last resort, and it looked like we had not got there yet.'

He unholstered it and flipped open the barrel, tipping out the bullets in one slick move, and then spun the barrel closed with a jerk of his wrist. With a wink he handed his revolver to Bea.

Bea wedged it into her waistband, stepped over to the mob of raptors and tried to shoo them away, but without success. They all looked around to Carter, who clicked a noise out of the side of his mouth making them disperse immediately. Hayter was scratched to bits, his arms covering his face, and he was whimpering.

'Thank you, thank you!' he called out, but when he looked up he realised who had finally saved him. 'You?'

'Yes, me. Get up.'

Hayter looked around at the numbers of raptors and people surrounding him and then let out a huff. He rolled onto all fours to compose himself before dragging himself up to his feet.

'What do you want?'

Hayter still sounded defiant. Bea held her hands on her hips and let the gun catch the light, sending a sharp ray of reflection into his eyes. Hayter went to shield them and Bea stepped forward, but as she did so he suddenly lurched towards her, snatching the gun. His other hand grabbed her wrists and he spun her around, holding the gun at her head.

'Stand back everyone.' Hayter chuckled to himself. 'You all must think I'm stupid.'

Theodore played along and held out both his hands.

'Steady now, Christian. This has gone too far – that's a young girl you have there.'

Bea gave Theodore a hard look. 'I'm thirteen years OLD, not young.'

Theodore started to laugh but suppressed it, not wanting to give the game away.

However the crowd was aghast and Carter went to lunge at Hayter, before Theodore grabbed him and pulled him back.

'No, Carter, he has a gun. Let's find out what he wants.'

Hayter smiled and re-opened his split lip. Spitting blood onto the ground he laughed out loud.

'I had your stupid plan sussed in minutes. The boy and his great-uncle's kylos – ha! What a joke. The bogus telegram – nice try. And then the explosives set around the depot . . . well, my best man is stripping it all down as we speak.'

A saliva blood bubble spurted from the corner of his mouth as Hayter laughed grimly. Suddenly a bright flash filled the sky, followed by a deafening boom that shook everything around them and startled the birds from the trees. A moment later a sonic wave of debris and dust shot down the street and onto the dock. In that stunned moment Bea pushed away from Hayter as everyone stared up at a black mushroom cloud growing above the depot at the end of the town, darkening the sky. With their ears still ringing, one by one everyone turned to face Hayter who had caught the brunt of the blast and was now looking more like a dusty ghost.

The postmistress stepped in.

'You were saying something about a joke? Tell me, did you get mine? The surgical spirit – or was it vinegar? I can't remember – you know the bottles are so similar. And the bicarbonate of soda to fix your tummy – or was it my foot powder? Bet that tasted real good.'

Hayter raised the gun at her. 'You will not live long enough to regret that.'

'Go on, shoot me.' She faced up to the man she hated with a passion.

'Stand back, or I will shoot you all!' Hayter spun around the crowd of people.

Bea took Carter's hand to try to make him understand that everything was actually all right before she made her next move.

'Go on, then!' Bea stood forward.

'Then me.' Bunty stepped in.

Hayter grinned. 'It will be my pleasure.'

The postmistress pushed in. 'Now step behind me, ladies, I was first – no one's getting shot before me.' She tutted her teeth, crossed her arms and looked Hayter up and down with disrespect.

'Good, then you will be first!' Hayter laughed.

Shuggy emerged from behind his mother's dress and walked forward.

'No, sir, I am first.'

'Shuggy! You always have to go and spoil things! Get back here, I tell you!' the postmistress shouted.

But he was defiant as he stood there grinning at Hayter.

'Any more want to get shot?' Hayter laughed again to himself.

'Yes, please.' Biggie stepped up, panting from his run back down the street.

'Biggie, you're safe!' Theodore shouted. 'Perfect timing, old friend, we're having a great time. Our good friend Christian here is offering to shoot us all with an unloaded gun.'

Hayter glanced down at the revolver and spun the empty barrel.

'My men have plenty more bullets,' he bluffed. He glared at Biggie. 'It was your dynamite, wasn't it? I would not be upsetting me right now, if I were you. My men have your son.'

Hayter had played his one and only trump card and suddenly the power of balance changed. Bea turned and saw Theodore's worried face.

'Excuse me, excuse me, coming through, make way, make way!'

The crowd that encircled Hayter parted, and in strolled Sammy, leading Junior.

'What have I missed? Busy Bee, I hope you have not been causing trouble again!'

Bea smiled back delightedly. Everyone cheered the young hero's return. Piled high on Junior's back, and bound in netting, were all of Hayter's men, each peppered with little blow darts. Biggie proudly picked up his son and hugged him.

'You been messing up my plan, Mr Glowgan?' Theodore could do nothing but smile and nod at the boy's perfect timing.

'Now, Mr Hayter, you're getting on that cargo boat with your friends and leaving this island for good, you hear?' The postmistress spoke with authority.

'You don't get to make decisions, I do.' Hayter answered quickly, brushing her aside, still trying to assert his position.

'Well, let's let the people decide.' The postmistress looked at the entire population of New Town who were gathered around. 'People, this is an emergency town meeting. Hands up if you want me to be the mayor!'

With that everyone's hand shot up except Shuggy's.

'Shuggy, this is a free election and I respect your vote, but when I get home you're –'

Shuggy was struggling with something in his hands but as everyone was now looking at him he stopped what he was doing and quickly held up his hand that was jammed in the jar of ginger.

'Good. A unanimous vote. So I am running things around here now,' said the postmistress, 'and I am asking you – in fact, I'm telling you – to leave this island with immediate effect!'

Hayter was finally lost for words.

32

Defiant Until the Very End

~ and that was that ~

Biggie made good use of the cages in the cargo boat and padlocked them all, taking care to chuck the keys overboard. Their new occupants were all snoring happily except for Christian Hayter; unluckily for him all the big cages had been taken and the next one down was half the size. The crew of the boat had been paid handsomely in spice to take as long as they wanted to get to their final destination and not to be persuaded to break open the cages. Theodore scoured the boat and removed anything that could be used to either pick the locks or cut the bars so temptation was beyond them.

No one gathered to wave the boat off.

◆ ◆ ◆

The next day, Captain Wilbur Woods returned to Koto Baru to ferry his customers back to the mainland and got a big surprise. The whole island had gathered to wave them off, and the dock was abuzz with the good news that there was a new mayor making sweeping changes and bringing back a more traditional way of life.

Bea was the first one aboard the *Orca*, as she had promised herself a week ago, followed by her brother, who sat up front to watch his island home bob up and down. Theodore helped Bunty onto the steamer boat as he always did, and the skinny deckhand was happy to see just one old trunk to load.

'Captain Woods, you be careful with that.' Bunty tapped the trunk. 'That hopefully holds some of the answers we came here looking for.'

The captain did a quick head count and realised they had one extra passenger aboard, doing a double-take and raising his eyebrows at the boy's tattered feathers. Theodore smiled and turned to wave at the crowd gathered at the other end of the jetty.

On the dock, Biggie put his arms around Jara and Sammy. 'I hate goodbyes.' He gritted his teeth as a joyful tear rolled down his face.

Sammy twiddled the shell necklace Bea had given him and quietly promised himself never to wash the cheek where Bea had kissed him goodbye. He accepted the ten quid Theodore owed him, but insisted the hire of Junior was 'on the house'. The new Mayor/Postmistress/General Store Manager/Hotelier/Nurse beamed in the new hat that Bunty had given her from Grace's trunk and patted Shuggy on the head.

Suddenly there came a cold and blood-curdling roar that sent a shiver down everyone's spine. The crowd parted and there, in the treeline, stood the Beast staring down on them all. Everybody edged away, trying not startle it. The Beast looked ahead and up the jetty to the steamer that had just cast off, Carter standing at the helm, looking back towards the island.

The Beast looked again at the entire townsfolk and then back at the boat. Like a coiled spring the saur leapt forward and bolted past everyone, shooting up the jetty, the thick wooden boards creaking and breaking under every thundering footstep, the support posts shattering as the huge tyrant's weight was loaded onto them. Theodore saw what was incoming and held onto Bunty. Bea grabbed Carter's arm and twisted a rope around the other to help brace them.

The Beast was running out of jetty and Captain Woods put the *Orca* into full throttle to get away, but it was not enough. The tyrant leapt off the jetty and landed on the steamer's stern, pushing it down momentarily under the water line.

Everyone yelled as the boat rocked violently back and forth and then righted itself. The enormous saur tried to adjust its balance but slipped in doing so, landing in a crouched position that it thankfully opted to not get up from. Like Carter, this was its first time on a boat. The boy bounded over, as pleased as punch to be reunited with his new friend, and patted its nose.

Watching them, Theodore got his kit bag open and rummaged around.

'Better put out some lines and get fishing! We'll need to keep him well fed so he doesn't get tempted by anybody onboard.' He turned to the startled captain. 'Room for one more?'

'I'm gonna need a bigger boat,' the captain muttered, and headed the *Orca* out to sea.

And that was that.

◆ ◆ ◆

The end is not the end, just as the beginning was not the beginning.

33

Nervous of the Boy

~ wearing feathers on a boat ~

After everyone was settled and the Islands of Aru became just a speck on the horizon, Captain Woods pulled Theodore to one side.

'I'm a little nervous of the boy.'

Theodore squinted at the captain. 'More than that tyrant?'

'No, it's the feathers. Wearing feathers on a boat, it attracts bad luck.'

Theodore went over to Carter who was standing up front on his own, letting the sea breeze fill his outstretched arms and fluttering his remaining feathers.

'How about we take off this cloak and get you into something more . . . human?'

Theodore smiled to show the boy he was being friendly, but just as he went to offer his jacket a large shadow loomed overhead.

Before anyone could do anything, Carter was lifted off the deck by a huge oceanic pterosaur. Theodore leapt up, grabbed hold of Carter's ankles and yanked. The strapping holding his feather cloak gave way and both of them fell backwards onto the deck.

Carter jumped up to his feet and looked up to the pterosaur that circled overhead with a mouth full of his feathers before gracefully settling on the sea.

Bea ran over to Carter and followed his gaze as the saur flipped Carter's old feathers into the air, then swallowed them.

'Don't worry, you won't need those where we are going.' Bea comforted her brother.

The water under the pterosaur grew dark and a giant mosasaur broke the surface, its mouth open wide revealing awesome rows of large teeth. It swallowed the pterosaur whole. Bea and Carter looked at each other and gulped.

In her cabin, Bunty placed Carter's remaining cloak of feathers and headband in his mother's trunk for safekeeping and dug out an old shirt and shorts that belonged to his father. The trunk contained many secrets from the past to unlock but, for now, everyone had one greater concern: their future together.

◆ ◆ ◆

THE END

APPENDIX

Excerpts from
Saurs of the Wild

~ by Nigel Winsor ~

DROMAEORAPTOR
Omnivore | Biped

Dromaeraptors are now commonly know as 'raptors'. The early dromaeoraptors were formidable hunters with a fierce reputation. Judging by numerous remains discovered around the world, dromaeoraptors were once widespread but have now mostly been eradicated. Only a small fraction of less aggressive raptors still exist in the wild. Gene sequencing has shown that these raptors descended from early domesticated dromaeoraptors, and selective breeding has contributed to the reduction of aggression in the species, but sadly their ancestors' once-feared reputation lives on and many are killed on sight by humans without hesitation.

Raptors are agile bipeds with serrated teeth, narrow snouts and forward-facing eyes on relatively large heads supported by S-curved necks. They have short, deep torsos, and a prominent pubic bone projecting beneath the base of their slender stiffened tails. Long arms are often folded against the body, large hands with three long fingers ending in sharp claws. Characteristically their feet feature an enlarged second toe with a sickle-shaped claw held off the ground in a hyper-extended 'retracted' position when walking, with only the third and fourth toes bearing the weight of the animal.

RAPTORS OF PARADISE

The group of saurs known as the Raptors of Paradise are considered to be 'true' dromaeoraptors – living in isolation on Papua and some of the surrounding remote islands has meant that the species seen in this part of the world have been free from selective breeding or human interference. Here, with no natural predators and an abundance of small mammals to feed on, these saurs have evolved characteristics not seen in other raptors. Females are typically brown in colour and their appearance is unremarkable, but male Raptors of Paradise have colourful, ornate feathers and elaborate courtship rituals for mating: aggression appears to have been naturally selected out. Sadly, their numbers are in rapid decline caused by the trade in their exotic feathers.

Blue Horned Raptor of Paradise (Bluepan)

The Blue Horned Raptor of Paradise, also known as a Bluepan, is found only on the remote Islands of Aru in Indonesia. It is one of just three types of raptor that possess fleshy horns and a wattle that males extend during courtship rituals. Male Bluepans are usually dark red with blue, black and white spots, a vivid pale blue face with white circles around their black eyes, and a short bib-like wattle that hangs below its neck. Female Bluepans have brown feathers and comical white circle marking around their eyes. The Bluepan opens its mouth wide and inflates its wattle and fleshy horns as part of its mating ritual. It was once believed that the wattle and horns were inflated by gulping in air, but research now shows that the Bluepan gulps air to stimulate the production of saliva and by shaking its head rapidly releases both saliva and blood to engorge the fleshy protrusions. The horns extend above the eyes and the wattle unravels to reveal a spectacular pattern of markings: dark blue and violet markings down its centre, with bright scarlet down each side.

Golden Fantailed Raptor of Paradise

The Golden Fantailed Raptor of Paradise is native to the rainforests of Papua and some of the surrounding islands, but due to the live export trade feral populations have also established themselves in some parts of Canada, the United States of America, Australia, the United Kingdom and throughout the forests of western Europe. Males are mostly covered in golden feathers with a scarlet red chest and deep blue forelimb feathers, and also sport a yellow wattle and legs. Their ruff or cape is light orange with deep blue flecks and can be raised for display. As is typical, the female is much less showy, with a mottled brown plumage but the same yellow legs.

Golden Fantail feathers became fashionable during the early part of the twentieth century but the cruel methods used in acquiring them were soon condemned. Legislation introduced in the 1930s changed the trade and it became fashionable to own a live raptor rather than wear the feathers of a dead one. To fulfil demand, exporters sold breeding pairs and soon many western households boasted a raptor or two in the garden. Many of these 'pet' raptors escaped or were deliberately released into the wild when they became less fashionable.

Raptors of Paradise:
1 Short-tailed
2 Long-tailed
3 Shadow
4 Fantailed
5 Blue Horned
6 Greater

Many adapted well to their new environments and interbred with indigenous wild raptors, creating hybrids such as the Common Bambiraptor in the United Kingdom and the iconic American Golden Raptor.

Greater Raptor of Paradise

The Greater Raptor of Paradise is one of the largest true members of the species. Males can measure up to 1.7 metres in the body, excluding the distinctive twin tail feathers that can double its length. The female is smaller, at only a metre long. The male Greater Raptor has maroon feathers covering its body and a vivid lime green head and nape, and this colouring extends to its forelimb feathers, which are lime green on the ends and underneath, so that they flap and flash in courtship. Its maroon tail feathers are streaked with white and pale blue, and end in two prominent extended feathers that are very supple and trail behind it like long ribbons. The Greater Raptor constantly whips these from side to side and over its head. Females are unremarkable in comparison, with a plain maroon body of short feathers. In both sexes, however, Greater Raptors have distinctive bright yellow irises and blue bills.

In Papua, chasing Greater Raptors is regarded as both a sport and a rite of passage for young indigenous tribesmen. The aim is to pluck a ribbon feather to wear as part of their ornate headdress. In the wild the long ribbon-like tail feathers often get snagged on tree roots or branches, so these raptors have evolved to allow the prominent tail feathers to fall out easily and grow back remarkably fast. This has kept the wild population healthy as their two most valuable assets are easily replaced.

There are a few smaller varieties of raptors that sport similar long ribbon tails, such as the endangered White Whipped Raptor of Paradise, with its jet-black body and bright white tail, and the Horse-tailed Raptor of Paradise, whose tail feathers have separated filaments that resemble a horse's tail.

Shadow Raptor

Little is known about the habits of the reclusive Shadow Raptor, the largest in its species. Distinct from other Raptors of Paradise, both male and female Shadow Raptors are covered in the same plumage. These unique feathers enable them to become extremely well camouflaged in their natural surroundings. Most notable are the dozen or so long display feathers that can be fanned out from behind its head and the curved feathers attached to its ankles that point outwards and upwards. These leg feathera have the dual function of disguising its movement and sweeping the floor of its nesting site and display arena.

Similar to early dromaeoraptors, Shadow Raptors have longer legs in proportion to their body than any other raptor. Having this extra height helps them move across the rainforest floor with ease. They are carnivores, and having caught their prey adopt a sitting position, using their long back legs to hold it still, leaving their sharp foreclaws to cut away at the flesh. What also separates them from other Raptors of Paradise is their aggression, leading many people to consider that Shadow Raptors are probably the closest living example of true dromaeoraptors.

Short-tailed Raptor of Paradise

Short-tailed Raptors of Paradise have stunted short heads crowned by a set of long fine feathers that continue down the chest and upper legs. This plumage can be either forward-facing or back-combed. The forelimb and tail feathers are unusually wide and short, decorated with a large coloured circle pattern often resembling an eye. In courtship these tail feathers are fanned out vertically, producing a perfect semi-circle. The Short-tailed Raptor can rotate its forelimbs further forwards than any other raptor, enabling it to produce a second semi-circle made from two quarter-fans of the long fine feathers of each forelimb. With its head in the centre of these semi-circles, it becomes hard to distinguish the front from the back of the raptor, who enhances this visual illusion by spinning around on the spot. When retracted, the wide tail feathers hang low under the tail. Due to the popularity of trade in their feathers it is now hard to find them in the wild, but they exist in abundance in captivity where they have also been interbred. Some of the cross-breed varieties have twin circles on their feathers and the Valentine Short-tailed Raptor boasts distinctive heart-shaped markings.

HADROSAUR

Herbivore | Biped/semi-quadrupedal

Hadrosaurs have characteristically flat duck-like beaks, large heads on flexible necks and elongated bodies that seamlessly continue into long stiff tails. They are able to run on their large hind legs, yet graze on all four. Their hind feet have three widely spread toes, and their strong forearms feature four 'fingers': three of uniform size and one smaller, often spiked.

Mature males boast distinctive and unusual bony crests on their heads. These perform the important functions of sound amplification for communication and thermoregulation. Hadros are comfortable in a habitat with plentiful fresh water, as their herbivorous diet is made up from large quantities of vegetation. However, some sub-families of hadros have adapted to living in a salt-water environment or manage to survive in deserts and dry arid plains. In domestic situations the passive and tame nature of most hadros has made them a popular saur to live alongside humans. In many developing parts of the world their dung is prized as a fertiliser, building material and as fuel.

Mittenhead Hadros
The Mittenhead Hadros was aptly named by early western travellers to Southeast Asia. The male's bony head crest has two twisted protrusions: the first larger and flatter, the second shorter and cylindrical. The overall effect is just like a mitten. In Asia, where the climate is temperate, mittens are unknown, so they are known by different names throughout the region. Mittenheads are widespread in Indochina and Indonesia and the size and shape of the 'mitten' crest differs in each sub-family. Female Mittenheads are almost indentical in body size, pattern and colouring to the males but lack the distinctive crest. Groups always feature a pair of alpha males with a harem of up to thirty females. Strangely, each of the paired males' crests will twist in opposite directions: one to the left and the other to the right. It is not known why this natural phenomenon occurs.

KYLOSAUR
Herbivore | Quadruped

Kylosaurs characteristically have broad tank-like bodies partially covered with an array of irregular bony plates. These plates protrude outwards into 'horns' along the outer edges of the body. Their broad heads feature bony beaks, and they commonly have two horns angled towards the back of the head and two horns below these that point downwards. The parts of their bodies without plates on the outside have round bony osteoderms under the skin, making a kylos the most heavily armoured saur of all. Larger varieties, such as Pricklebacks and Hornbacks, have an enlarged mass of bone forming a club at the end of their tails used both for defence and to create a pendulum motion to aid locomotion. By swinging the club from side to side a rocking momentum helps lift its heavy bulk. Slender varieties like Leatherbacks and Sidespines don't need club tails to help them move their lighter bodies and have longer spikes in their more vulnerable parts that offer sufficient defence. Kylos have hoof-like toes on all four legs, although its front legs are slightly shorter than its hind legs.

Kylosaurs come in many forms and were once spread throughout the world. Many ancient civilisations used their thick hides and bony plates as armour. Numerous descriptions and drawings depicting huge armies clad in kylos armour led scholars to believe that these formidable saurs were once revered. With a capacity to eat on the move, travel great distances, withstand hardship and endure extreme conditions these beasts of burden were used for transporting heavy goods.

With the introduction of wheeled carts that could be pulled by horses, the use of kylos became less frequent, resulting in many species becoming almost extinct. Today they can still be found working alongside man in places where horses and carts are impractical, or carrying extremely heavy loads that horses or pack donkeys would struggle with.

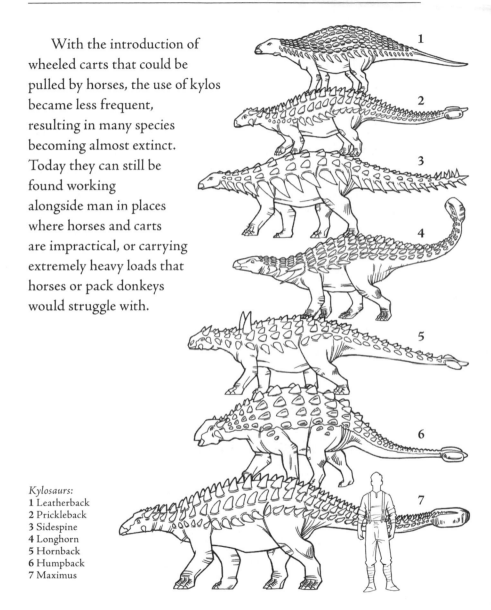

Kylosaurs:
1 Leatherback
2 Prickleback
3 Sidespine
4 Longhorn
5 Hornback
6 Humpback
7 Maximus

MIMUSAUR
Omnivore | Biped

Mimusaurs are lightly feathered saurs with powerful hind legs and three short, strong weight-bearing toes on each long foot, terminating in hoof-like claws. They have long and slender necks, bird-like heads with large eyes on each side and toothless beaks. Most have three long powerful claws on each slender forelimb used for hooking down branches on which to feed. Mimus' herbivorous diet is occasionally supplemented with small prey when the opportunity arises. These saurs are very social animals, often living naturally in large groups.

Around the world, mimusaurs have been bred for a variety of uses as they are easy to train to follow simple commands, are calm around humans and cost very little to keep and maintain. However, like all omnivores and herbivores, they are unpredictable around carnivorous saurs and either freeze to the spot and quiver uncontrollably or bolt in fear. Many owners opt to use blinkers to

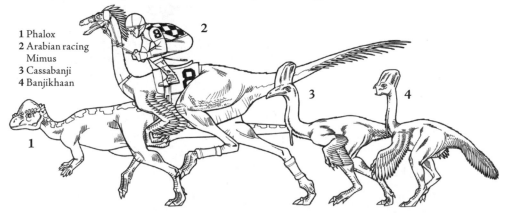

1 Phalox
2 Arabian racing
  Mimus
3 Cassabanji
4 Banjikhaan

shield their mimus' eyes from looking backwards, and some train them to 'bury their heads' under their forelimb feathers until any potential scare has passed.

Today the sport of mimus racing is having a resurgence in parts of the world, enjoyed on the same occasions as the more established pastime of horse racing. For centuries the two sports were strictly separated; depending on your family roots you were either a horse or mimus fan and fiercely supported your inherited sport. Troubles would constantly arise between events and it was a common excuse for brawls and family feuds. During the First World War, however, the training and sport of both these docile creatures was combined for a greater cause. After the war, keeping horses became more popular as they could also be used in agriculture and thus mimus racing fell into decline.

Silva Mimus

With their excellent balance, Silva Mimus are perfectly suited for riding in dense woodland and tropical forests. Steep inclines and slopes are easily traversed where horses and donkeys would be slow or might stumble. Silva Mimus are able to carry moderate loads for long distances, work well in packs and eat on the move.

OVIRAPTOR
Biped | Omnivore

Oviraptors are feather-covered bird-like saurs with characteristically short, parrot-like beaks, often with bony crests atop their head. Typically oviraptors have long forearms (though this varies considerably in some of the species) with two long clawed fingers and a much smaller third finger. Most varieties of oviraptor have a thick set of elongated display feathers over their arms with shorter feathers covering the body and long, sturdy scaly legs with three wide weight-bearing toes on each foot. Their short tails often end with four fused vertebrae that serve as the attachment point for their fan of tail feathers. Some eat small vertebrates or molluscs to support their mainly herbivorous diet.

Banjikhaan (Banji)

The Banjikhaan, more popularly known as banji, is a small light-built forest-dwelling oviraptor. It originates from Northern China but its habitat has spread due to the sea-trade and it has now become an invasive species on many small islands around the world. Both male and female banji have red beaks, long bright yellow wattles and, in some cases, elaborate coloured crests. Usually their body feathers are bright green or turquoise, with some rare groups displaying vivid blue feathers. Females are slightly larger, with a more brightly coloured crest in those groups that display one.

In the tropical forests of New Guinea, nearby islands and parts of Northeastern Australia, the Cassabanji has evolved to resemble the Southern Cassowary that also populate these regions. With its enlarged colourful middle crests on its head, long pink wattles and stunted tail, the resemblance is useful for the saur, as the flightless bird has a fierce reputation and is known to attack humans. It was once believed that the cassowary was a saur, but it was reclassified as a flightless bird in the twentieth century.

Unlike other oviraptors, who lay elongated eggs in flat nests, banji dig large deep nests in the soft moist forest ground, partially burying them to help with incubation; this results in their eggs being perfectly rounded. Banji meat is considered a delicacy in China, and in Mongolia it forms the central dish of the feast of Khaan. Elsewhere in the world its meat is not considered fit for consumption as it has a bitter taste. Today banji numbers are in decline, as the remote islands that they once dominated became more populated by humans and other domesticated animals, such as dogs, who dig up their unguarded nests to eat the eggs. Raising chickens has also became more popular, as they offer both tasty eggs and meat, and require less feed and care to maintain. The Brown Banji that was once found all over New Zealand is now critically endangered, and the diminutive Redhead Banji can no longer be found in the wild.

PHALOX
Herbivore | *Biped*

Phalox typically have thick domed or flat wedge-shaped heads surrounded by nodes or spikes used for both display and defence. Their long hind limbs have three weight-bearing toes and their small forelimbs have five fingers. Their broad strong tails aid balance and make them well suited to the rugged mountainsides and high altitudes of their natural habitat.

Nomadic by choice, phalox don't get along very well with other animals and are naturally fierce, with daily challenges in the wild for supremacy amongst both male and female to secure the day's alpha leader. The shape of their skulls and their U-shaped necks prevent effective head-on strikes. Heads are instead side-swiped at each other and the resonating sound can be heard for many miles around. The victor is usually the one who makes the loudest noise, and this is not necessarily the phalox who can hit hardest. In mating season huge numbers of wild phalox gather for bouts of head-butting, which creates a deafening noise for days on end.

Domesticated phalox are used throughout the world as their ability to carry great loads over long distances compensates for their antisocial behaviour towards other animals. This naturally unfriendly temperament means they are excellent guard saurs for villages and property as they are fast to respond and unrelenting in their persistence to fend off unwanted intruders. Where guard dogs will bark, and a bite may break the skin of its opponent, a guard phalox will charge and butt, and can break the bones of a fully grown man in one blow. They are understandably feared and take careful handling by their owners.

Through selective breeding, domesticated phalox no longer need to butt heads daily in the pack as they do in the wild but they still must be treated in a similar way to their wilder cousins by their human owners, who must challenge them every morning (and win) to be the day's alpha leader. Usually a metal bucket butted on the phalox's domed bony head will resonate loudly enough to 'win', but sometimes full-blown challenges must take place where extreme caution is needed. Every phalox herdsman has a tale of being put in his place for the day and humbly bowing to the victor, his charge. Most would need to seek medical attention of some kind as a result of losing the challenge.

RHAMP RHAT
Omnivore | Aerial

There are over 1,000 known varieties of Pterosaurs around the world and the group of Rhamp Rhats are probably one of the oldest and misunderstood flying creatures. Many mainstream religions have come to demonise rhats as 'flying demons' but indigenous peoples tend to think of rhats as extremely lucky, as they eat pests and mosquitoes. They are also a delicacy with many tribesfolk, so you are considered fortunate to catch one as a tasty treat. Rhats are often mistaken for ghats but there are two simple ways to spot the difference. Rhats have long tails and needle-like teeth that splay forwards and sometimes outwards. Ghats are all short-tailed with small rows of teeth. Commonly rhats have long pointed beaked snouts (with the exception of Womp Rhats, a small sub-family with a backward horn) and ghats mostly have short, wide heads, except for the well documented group of Galapagos Ghats, which have toothless sharp beaks.

Rhiptus Rhat

The Rhiptus Rhat can be mostly found in Indonesia, Papua and Northern Australia. Some small colonies are also known to live in Japan and were thought to have been introduced to combat the mosquito epidemic in the early nineteenth century. They have a characterful upward-turned beaked snout, comical splayed teeth and large eyes that help it see in the low light of dark forests and jungles. With an average 200cm wingspan, the Rhiptus Rhat is one of the largest sub-tropical rhats due to its rich diet of flying insects as it feeds on the wing. Its short feathered skin is fur-like in appearance and helps to repel rain, and its wing membrane is lightly iridescent and patterned. Most notable is the Rhiptus's long stiff tail with colourful diamond-shaped vane.

Common Rhat

The Common Rhat, measuring an average 60cm wingspan, is one of the smallest rhats in the world, and is mostly found living in small woodlands or agricultural buildings near farmyards, as their diet mostly consists of flies that are attracted to cows or other farmed animals. European Rhamp Rhats are usually grey, with a wide and blunt-beaked snout well suited to its diet. Its long stiff tail has a small dark oval vane at its end. The European Rhamp Rhat has often interbred with the Brown Rhat, which is mostly brown, and produced the better-known Common Rhat, which is a mottled mix of the two colourings. Due to the decline in smallholdings and traditional farming methods, the European and Brown Rhat have been in steady decline and now legislation in several European countries protects their nesting sites. In addition, these rhats can suffer badly from red mite picked up from farmyard chickens. The mites infest their nests, causing irritation to the skin. Scratching themselves vigorously with their sharp pin-like teeth causes the rhat's feathers to fall out and partially bald infants may not make it through their first winter.

1 Womp Rhat
2 Oceanic Pterosaur
3 Common Rhat
4 Rhiptus Rhat
5 Barn Ghat
6 Stubnose Rhiptus

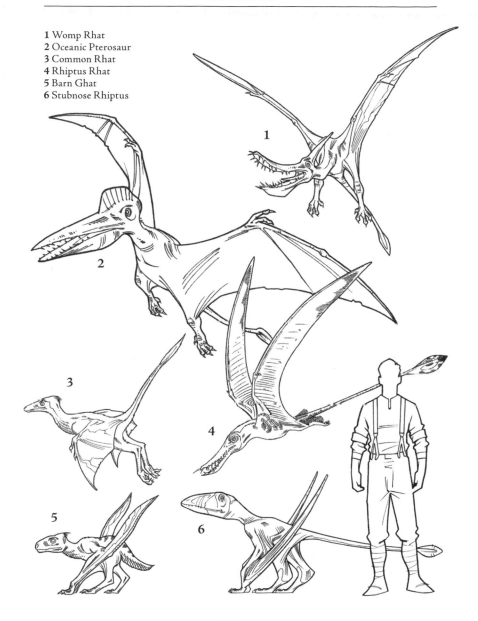

TRITOP
Herbivore | Quadruped

Tritops are sturdy quadrupeds with a thick tail and short, strong limbs; they have three hooves on each forefoot, and four hooves on each hind foot. What makes them unmistakable are the elaborate horns and bony frills covering their necks, which are used for display, defence and heat regulation. The orientation, configuration, colour and size of their horns and frills shows remarkable variation between the sub-species. Most tritops have either long, triangular frills and well-developed brow horns, or shorter and more rectangular frills with elaborate spines and well-developed nasal horns. The majority live in large grazing herds and have complicated social structures and ranked hierarchies. Due to their succulent meat and versatile hides, it is believed that these were the first animals to be domesticated for use as livestock by early humans, and some of the oldest neolithic cave paintings depict tritops in hunting scenes. Selective breeding has created tritop hybrids better suited for meat and leather production, as well as for use in a variety of sports and as agricultural labour.

Silver Shorthorn

The Silver Shorthorn is one of the smaller tritops and the most common variety found in Indonesia today. Their comparatively small build, horns and frill, combined with their placid nature, make them easy to keep in island communities where fences are not common. The Silver Shorthorn originated in Java, as a result of interbreeding between the larger indigenous Silverskin and the popular Western Shorthorn. This produced a smaller tritop with the palatable meat of the Western Shorthorn whilst still boasting the Silverskins' prized hide, used in a wide variety of clothing and household goods.

Silver Shorthorns are often kept as a pair, and will produce around six to eight eggs every eighteen months. Both male and female help to raise the young on a diet of coarse vegetation, and the juveniles are usually slaughtered at around eighteen months old to make room for the next hatch of eggs. Official legislation recently banned the practice of starving the juveniles for two weeks prior to slaughter so that their skin becomes easier to strip away from the carcass but remote places where the Silver Shorthorn is farmed continue to use this barbaric method.

TYRANT
Carnivore | Biped

These carnivores have short, muscular S-shaped necks to support their massive heads, and strong jaws able to exert the largest bite-force of any terrestrial animal. They have a wide barrel chest, sturdy hind legs with three weight-bearing toes (among the longest in proportion to body size of any saur) and balanced by a long, heavy tail. They have short but powerful forelimbs with two clawed fingers. To compensate for its immense bulk, many bones throughout the tyrant's skeleton are hollow, reducing weight without significant loss of strength. Some tyrants, known as ceratyrants, have bony, horn-like protrusions on their heads, and tyrants can vary in size; dwarf tyrants are comparatively diminutive.

Black Dwarf Tyrant

The Black Dwarf Tyrant is by far the smallest known tyrant, with fully grown adults measuring a maximum eight metres long. It is believed to have originated on the small island of Flores in Indonesia; fossil remains on many nearby islands prove that they were once great swimmers, with long necks enabling them to keep their heads above water with ease. The present-day descendants spend more time on land, where they fish in shallow waters and do not stray past the surrounding reefs. Their forearms have extra skin extending from wrist to shoulder, which enables the Dwarf Black to better use its arms when swimming, and their elongated tail feathers also help propel itself in water.

Dwarf Black Tyrants have an unusual dominant gene that causes hyperpigmentation (fibromelanosis). This means its skin, feathers, claws, bones and internal organs appear dark black. Its blood and tongue are unaffected,

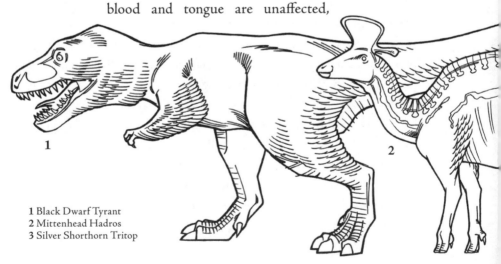

1 Black Dwarf Tyrant
2 Mittenhead Hadros
3 Silver Shorthorn Tritop

although both are remarkably dark. It is thought that at some point in its isolated evolution these tyrants interbred, causing the hyperpigmentation mutation. The Black Dwarf's fish-heavy diet helps it produce natural oils, which it secretes from its skin. This preen oil binds and nourishes the black feathers, creating a protective waterproof layer that also repels the many sandflies and biting insects that gather close to the shoreline. The oiled feathers give off a reflective iridescent sheen that protects the skin beneath the tyrant's feathered coat from ultraviolet light. This gives the Dwarf Black the fearsome appearance of a stocky heavily-oiled bodybuilder glistening in a spectrum of dense colour.

Black Dwarf Tyrants make a distinctive nervous chattering sound, created by rattling its lower jaw from side to side and salivating whilst inhaling. It is not known why they do this but early settlers to the islands believed they were devils banished from hell and were shivering from being constantly cold, even in the tropical climate.

+ + +

3

NORTH

AMERICA

NORTH

ATLANTIC

NORTH

PACIFIC

OCEAN

SOUT

ERICA

ATLANT

PACIFIC

OCEAN

OCEA

ANTARCTIC

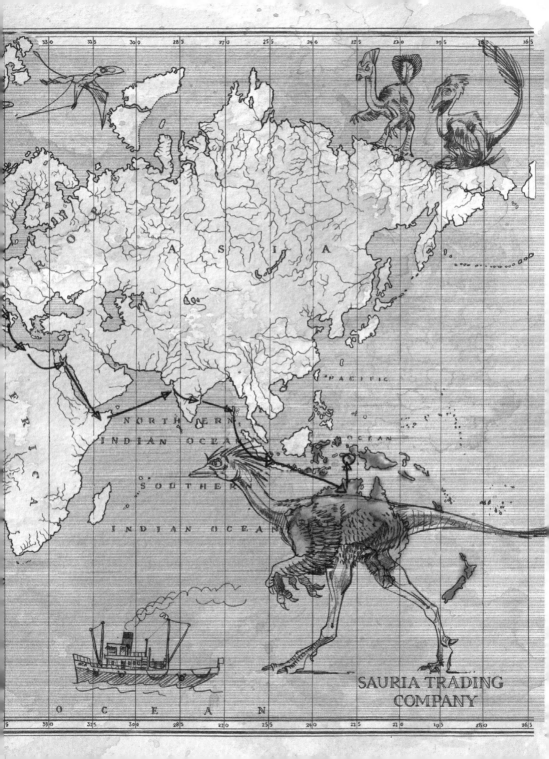

SAURIA TRADING
COMPANY

ACKNOWLEDGEMENTS

Everyone I know or who has somehow influenced me deserves a thank you for shaping me to be the person I am; without that Supersaurs would never have been dreamed up. And without the direct help I received from the following people, Supersaurs would still be rattling around in my head. Thank you to:

Chris West for jumping on the ship a long time ago and helping me visualise the world. He would like to thank Patsy, Sophia and Jasmin for all their love, support and endless cups of tea.
   Matt Nicholls without whom none of this would have been possible.
   Jamie Sully for fixing everything together and making it legit.
   Jeremy Davies for being the second person to put his hand up.
   Jack Dyson and Matt Kopinski for helping the words flow out.
   Jon Elek and Nicholas Lovell for their guidance and enthusiasm.
   The amazing team at Preloaded who helped develop and build the app.
   Mark Smith and all at Bonnier Zaffre who have helped make the adventure happen, especially my amazing editor, Emma Matthewson.

Love, support and encouragement came in huge quantities over the years from these people:
   My wonderful wife Mel, and our boys Cash and Carter, who fill my life.
   My Burridge family: Barbara, Roger, Patricia, Cody, Bev, Sienna and Carmen.
   My Myers family: Micki, Matthew, Lucia, Javier, Jackson, Kate, Lola and Toni.
   The Moss/Woods/Logan families: The Judge, Lisa, Caitlin, Mimi, Becca, Toby, Wilbur, Bennett, Nick, Caz, Freddie, Gail and Ian, Harriet, Mark and the boys, Barnaby, Sam, Lana and the original Theo Logan.
   Matt, Lou, Guy, Bea and Honor Nicholls. Jase, Elly, Cass and Noah Flemyng, Minnie and Henry Driver; Shane, Nigel, Kate and Phillip Winser. Pete, Laura, Archie, Kit and Annie Williams. Amy, Tim, Nell and Jago Bevan. Mike, Mel, Bonnie, Lulu and Carmella Keat. Claire, Bob, Audrey and Louis Sakoui. And my countryshire friends: the Crossleys, the Van-Cutsems, the Delevingne-Grants, Martin Goodyear and Tania Rotherwick.
   Jamie Oliver for his unending support and friendship and for taking a crazy idea and turning it into a Dinersaur Diner. Steve Lazarides, The Captain, Sailorboy, Nurse Millie, Fabian Fritze and the whole team who helped build the exhibition in LA.
   Finally to Huse Monfaradi, because a long time ago I said I would always give him a dedication whenever possible for no particular reason.

This book is dedicated to the wonderful Mike Myers and Mark Speight, who both sadly missed out on so much.

Jay Jay x